Between Two

For Annette

Between Two Seas

R D Cook

seren

Seren is the book imprint of
Poetry Wales Press Ltd
57 Nolton Street, Bridgend, Wales, CF31 3AE
www.seren-books.com

ISBN 978-1-85411-473-0

A CIP record for this title is available from the British Library.

Cover photograph: Phil Cope

Inner design and typesetting by books@lloydrobson.com

Printed by Cromwell Press Ltd, Trowbridge

The publisher works with the financial assistance of
the Welsh Books Council.

Mixed Sources
Product group from well-managed
forests and other controlled sources
www.fsc.org Cert no. TF-COC-2082
© 1996 Forest Stewardship Council
FSC

E

Endless
returning, endless
revolution of dream to ember, ember to anguish,
anguish to flame, flame to delight,
delight to dark and dream, dream to ember

– Denise Levertov
from *Relearning the Alphabet*

ONE

Tomas slept through four rings of the telephone, but when the answering machine clicked in and a distant, familiar voice spoke to him, his mind rose to the surface and he opened his eyes.

The room was dim, although the curtains weren't drawn over the narrow corner window, and the bedroom door stood open.

His head was pounding. Every heartbeat was causing black spots and streaks of brilliant light to flash and dance around the room.

Sitting up, he stared at the blood stain on his pillow; a dry, rusty blot almost the size of his head, and he felt a sickness in his stomach. He didn't dare touch the wound, which he knew was raw and swollen.

There could be no lying in bed now, even though his body insisted that he go back to sleep and forget the day. Somehow he would have to get to that interview with Jenna Mundey.

His clothes were neatly folded on the chair, socks and trainers underneath. He swung his legs round and stood, cold and naked, on the bare floorboards. As he dressed he tried to distract himself from the dizziness by gazing out at the granite wall rising high behind the tiny back yard.

The jagged shapes of some of the stones looked like faces. One reminded him of the crowned head with three faces on the rood screen at St Credan's church in Sancreed. It was staring at him, accusingly, and he had to look away.

He picked up his watch from the desk by the window – it said eleven thirty-five – and strapped it to his wrist. Lorca would be here soon.

Tomas walked unsteadily to the bathroom, but as soon as he opened the door and saw the pale streaks of blood on the rim of the bath he slammed it shut again and went back to his room.

He opened the desk drawer where he usually kept his notebook, but it wasn't there. It wasn't in his chest of drawers either.

He picked up the manila folder lying on the desk and carried it down to the landing.

Leaning against the doorframe of his father's room, he scanned every surface. The floor was strewn with work clothes, aprons, boots and an empty rum bottle.

At the top of the stairs he grabbed hold of the handrail to keep himself from falling. One step at a time, he descended.

The red light on the answering machine in the living room was flashing. He pressed the play button and listened.

'Hi, Tomas, it's Lorca. Are you there?' A pause. 'I've got a problem. The bloody bike wouldn't start! I've just got it going, but I haven't even left Exeter. So I'm not going to get to you in time, am I? Are there any buses from Lamorna on Sundays? Or would your dad give you a lift to Grumbla... if you grovel? Or would he grumble?' He laughed. 'Sorry. Anyway, *it's only, what, five miles? You might have to walk it, mate. Sorry to let you down, but I won't get there and back today, and I've got a lecture first thing tomorrow. So I'll see the Birthday Boy on Tuesday. Okay? Hope all goes well with Mizz Mundey. I'll phone later to see how you got on.'*

Tomas thought the message was over, but after another pause, Lorca added, *'This is pathetic. We should get ourselves mobile phones. Tomas...? Happy Valentine's Day!'*

He went through to the kitchen, unbolted and opened the back door. The cold air was a slap in the face.

He cautiously made his way round to the back yard and leant his shoulder against the wall to steady himself while he pissed against it.

At the kitchen sink he turned on the cold tap and leant forward, ducking the back of his head under the stream and pulling the dark matted curls free of the wound. Patting his hair dry with the tea towel, he saw the pink stains and tossed it onto the lid of the rubbish bin.

He sat at the table. According to the clock on the wall, always ten minutes fast, it was nearly noon. He would have to walk to Grumbla. The two rambling bus journeys – one going the few miles into Penzance, then another the few miles out again – weren't an option on a Sunday. Anyway, the walk might do him good once he got going. If he didn't make it to the interview he probably wouldn't get another chance. It was too late to phone and cancel now. She would think he was being off-hand, which certainly wasn't the case. He'd been looking forward to meeting her all term.

Tomas continued to sit. Apart from feeling so ill, his inertia was worse because he had an irrational fear that if he got up and walked out of the door he might never come back.

He had become trapped, pushed into a corner, and could only escape by leaving for good or else retaliating, either of which would hurt his father. Although Tomas sometimes felt like hurting him in some way, he wasn't an aggressive person. He despised the bullying that went on even at college; the mindless drunken behaviour he always tried to avoid in pubs, and outside them in the streets and parks around Penzance. A recent by-law had banned people from drinking in public, but that hadn't stopped the aggro and he hated it.

The thought that his father might have taken his notebook caused last night's chaos to start seeping back.

He quickly opened his folder, took out a piece of paper and a pen and scribbled a note:

> *Did you take my notebook?*
> *I want it back.*
> *I'm going to Jenna Mundey's.*
> *Maybe somewhere else after that.*

His father would have to make his own bloody supper and eat alone for a change. He placed the note flat on top of the sugar bowl, where a winter fly had just been grooming itself.

Gripping the edge of the table, he stood up, grabbed his coat from the hook beside the back door and put it on. Despite the icy wind, he pulled the knitted gloves from his coat pocket and threw them angrily across the room. He would have to wear his cap though. His hair was long and dark, but it wouldn't completely hide the bloody lump on the back of his head.

He shuffled through the dim living room into the hallway, then remembered the folder and went back to get it. Passing the answering machine, he pushed the delete button.

After closing the front door and dropping the key into the jar on the porch shelf, Tomas realised that he hadn't shaved. Stroking the fine stubble on his chin, he supposed it wouldn't be all that noticeable. Anyway there wasn't time now.

There weren't any cars parked in front of their row of cottages, and only one in the harbour car park above the sea wall. Tomas looked out at the cove: the towering granite quay, dominant as a fortress; the high cliffs curving round to clutch the old port like a grasping claw; the mass of discarded quarry stones piled steeply on a ledge above the harbour, as if they were about to dislodge themselves and hurtle down to join all the others lying on the tiny strand. It had happened once – during the great December storm when Tomas was five. Gales had raged for two days and nights, battering the cliffs above the harbour and creating a landslide that had barely missed Cliff Cottage, just beyond their terrace. The tide had swelled, mounted the car park and pushed an old Morris Minor right up to their front door.

The hedges and walls of the little garden between the cottage and the strand were swept away and tons of boulders and debris left in their place.

It had been the most exciting day of his life. But soon afterwards, when the everyday routine of cove life had re-established itself, he felt a vague disappointment that had never really left him. Every storm after that, which he would always welcome, had been something of a failure.

Turning left he crossed the little brook flowing into the harbour, passed the public toilets and took the footpath that threaded up through the wooded valley.

Since childhood, at the start of every lone journey along this trail, Tomas would feel both exhilarated and daunted. It was the anticipation of an adventure, however small or mundane, leaving all the constraints of the cove and family life behind. But at the same time he would be struggling with a creeping anxiety that he might never experience total freedom in his life. Once he'd lost sight of the cottages below, those feelings would pass.

He knew this valley in every season, in all weathers, and it always seemed to acknowledge him, too. Today it was the ivy, slowly crawling up the broad trunks and along the branches of ash and sycamore, the closeness of the tender embrace becoming a smothering grip. There were the clusters of wild garlic blossoming in patches of rough open ground, which today reminded him of the smell on his father's clothes when he came home from his long day's work in the hotel kitchen. And the little daffodils, showing themselves in the muddy spaces between granite boulders – fragile, sensitive individuals, compared to the acres of gaudy yellow sheets blowing in the fields up by Boleigh Farm.

A dead branch of oak, fallen in a recent gale, was crushing some of the daffodils. Stopping to move it, he picked three damaged budding stalks, slipped them into his folder and walked on.

So this was St Valentine's Day. But who was Valentine? Some martyr, probably. Lorca had told him that the saint's relics were in a church in Dublin and, on every fourteenth of February, his gold casket was solemnly carried to the high altar during a special mass for young people – and anyone else who was in love, he supposed. There was always a good turn-out, Lorca told him.

Tomas knew what love was. He'd read lots of poems

about love and had written a few himself. It was a different kind of pain, he'd written, pulling at your core, insisting that you acknowledge its presence and the prospect of a life transformed.

Love riddled Shakespeare's sonnets, some of which he knew by heart:

> *My love is as a fever, longing still*
> *For that which longer nurseth the disease;*
> *Feeding on that which doth preserve the ill.*

His ponderings ended abruptly when the root of an oak tree caught his foot. He fell forward, barely managing to stretch out his arms to take the brunt of the fall. The impact jarred his head and he shouted out in pain, but there was no one to hear him.

Tomas sat up, stunned, his heart racing. He picked up his folder and finally got to his feet. Brushing himself down he realised with a jolt that he was wearing his dull, grey corduroy trousers and faded flannel shirt. And his trainers! He'd intended to dress smartly for his meeting with Jenna, maybe even wear the tie he'd bought – or been given – for the funeral.

Panicky and confused, he considered going back to change. But he was almost at Lamorna Gate, and he hadn't the time or the energy now.

He reached the head of the valley and was about to cross the lane when a white van came speeding round the bend and zoomed past without even noticing he was there.

'Arsehole!' he shouted after it.

If he'd stepped onto the road a moment sooner it would have hit him, and that would have been the end of it.

Having safely crossed to Trewoofe Wood, he felt dizzy

again and sat on a low tree stump fringed with a tutu of bracket fungus.

Would he make it to Grumbla? Yes, if he took it in stages, stopping along the way whenever he needed to rest and recover. There was time.

After the long stretch of stone hedge at Trenuggo, the footpath met the Penzance to Land's End road. He could see the top of *Tregonebris* – The Blind Fiddler – above the thorn hedge; standing alone and solemn in a corner of the field.

Tomas believed that by using its Cornish name, the Tregonebris Stone, he had established something of a good relationship with this tall, tapering megalith that had always frightened him as a child.

He went in through the farm gate, walked over to the stone and sat close beside it, sheltering out of the wind.

Hello, Old Man, he said without speaking.

He knew he should go back home. But feeling Tregonebris' massive granite body against his, he closed his eyes, concentrating on its power. Silently he asked for strength to get through the day.

He rested for a while, then pulled one of the daffodils from the folder to lay on the ground at the stone's broad base – not so much an offering, as an outright gift. But the stem caught on a fold in his list of interview questions, and a gust of wind lifted the sheet of paper straight up into the air. Finding a current, it sailed on a crisscross course across the field.

Tomas shouted, 'No!'

Standing too quickly, he felt a surge of giddy sickness and had to lean back against Tregonebris. The page rose higher and then disappeared over the hedge.

He watched for a moment longer, trying to convince

himself that it didn't really matter. He might be able to remember most of what he'd written because he'd studied all the questions his classmates had decided on, and spent hours rehearsing everything he wanted to ask.

Tomas didn't bother trying the door at Sancreed church. The morning service was over and the door would probably be locked. After a few minutes rest, sitting at the base of one of the ancient crosses in the churchyard, he carried on up the lane that skirted Sancreed Beacon.

There was nearly an hour to go. Time enough to make a detour. He crossed the lane to the footpath and read the sign posted there:

CORNISH SACRED SITES PROTECTION NETWORK
SANCREED HOLY WELL
Please take care not to cause accidental damage when visiting Ancient Sites. Any physical damage will also damage the spirit of the place – please respect the land and all its inhabitants; spirits, animals, plants and stones.
Don't change the site – let the site change you!

Tomas followed the footpath to a small copse at the top of the hill.

Beside the chapel ruin, its thick walls wrapped in lichen and ivy, was the tall stone cross. He read the words circling its base that were not obscured by ivy:

...of your charity pray for the sick, the sorrowful, the tempted...

Nearby was the ancient holy well. He'd come here once or twice as a boy, and several times during the terrible last months of his mother's illness. Since then, how many times? Many.

The granite vaulting above the well lay half hidden in a thicket of hedge. The spreading thorn tree, growing close beside the steep steps leading down into the well, was festooned with myriad strips of coloured rags and ribbons, which he always stopped to examine.

Some of these clouties were old, faded and tattered, others looked as though they had only recently been tied onto the branches.

Tradition said that as the prayer rag or cloutie decayed, the wish made at the well would be granted to its donor. Some of these strips had probably been left by New Age pilgrims. He sometimes encountered little troops of them in the lanes around West Penwith, particularly during the summer months. But he was sure that at least a few of these clouties had been left by local people – perhaps still convinced of the healing power of the well. Some were made of synthetic materials, so it was difficult to know how long they'd been hanging there. He thought how stupid it was to leave a strip of polyester or nylon as a token of respect for the spirit of the well.

One curious cloutie caught his eye: a long cord of sheep's wool, dyed a rich purple and braided together with strands of horsehair.

He went to the mouth of the well, took off his cap, then hesitated for a moment before descending the six granite steps into its stone-lined recess.

Within this dark chamber there was just room enough for him to stand upright above the basin of water. The walls glowed with a moss-green phosphorescence. He crouched down, careful to keep his head in an upright position.

Hello, Old Woman, he said without speaking. He hoped that this place would once again draw something fresh from some far corner of his mind. If so, it would come to him almost at once in the form of a verse. If not, he couldn't force it.

He reached into the basin of icy water, drew out a cupped handful and splashed it over his face. He bent his head forward and let another handful run over the ugly wound on the back of his head.

He sat back, closed his eyes and was immediately aware of some resistance, probably caused by the giddiness in his head. A vague conflict, a struggle between thoughts and feelings he didn't want to acknowledge, was taking place in his mind.

Tomas was about to stand up and leave when he felt a sudden shifting, a lightness, which at first he mistook for dizziness. But it wasn't. He placed both hands flat on the damp stone floor to steady himself, listened to his breathing and tried to empty his mind again.

Suddenly the verse came to him. It was a couplet of long lines: a complex combination of words – some of them jarring – not at all fluid when he repeated them aloud. He took a sheet of paper from his folder and wrote them down.

At first, seeing them on the page, he wondered whether they were actually his own words. Could they be from a poem he'd read in class, or from some anthology he'd taken out of the library? He decided they weren't, because he recognised, couched in the couplet, a presentiment of something that had been troubling him. The verse must refer to his father, maybe to his sister as well, though he hoped that it didn't.

Outside in the diffuse winter light, Tomas pulled on his

cap and turned to look at the thorn tree's clouties again. He took the second daffodil from the folder, wanting to tie it onto a branch. He decided to use the strand of purple cord to secure the flower with a loose bow-knot.

The narrow lane below Sancreed Beacon was empty. It seemed to him that its only purpose today was to keep the broad, russet expanse of bracken and heather on one side from crossing over to the rolling green pastures on the other.

Just before the little settlement at Grumbla he arrived at the drive. A slate sign on the post read: *Chyangwyns*. Another sign opposite was covered over with a black plastic bin bag.

He glanced up the drive to the farmstead, nearly half a mile away, blew on his hands and looked at his watch: 1:50. Curious about the covered sign, he lifted the bin liner and read: *Chyangwyns Guest House – Bed & Breakfast*.

As he was sliding the covering back into place, a vehicle pulled up behind him. He stepped onto the drive, waiting for it to pass. Instead, the Jeep Cherokee turned in and stopped. The driver opened his window.

The man's face was creased and weathered, with a stubble of grey beard. He wore a camouflage jacket, almost a perfect match with the vehicle, Tomas noticed – khaki and spattered with dry mud.

'What are you doing?' the man asked, brusquely.

'I'm going to see Jenna Mundey.'

'Expecting you, is she?'

'Yes.'

The man gave a low grunt, grabbed a paint-smeared tarpaulin from the passenger seat and threw it onto the floor behind him.

'Get in, then.'

The man reached across and opened the passenger door.

Tomas felt a surge of fear, stood back and shook his head.

'It's all right. I don't mind walking.'

The man stared at him. Without saying another word, he slammed the door and the Jeep accelerated at such speed the tyres whirred on the gravel before they caught.

Tomas tucked the folder under his elbow, jammed his hands into his coat pockets and walked on.

His reaction worried him. He'd been annoyed by the man's rough manner, but that didn't explain the panic he'd felt. Maybe it was because he was reminded of his father.

More than half way up the hill the drive met a rougher, unmade track on the right that probably went to the farm itself.

Tomas stopped to re-fasten the top button of his coat. Pulling down his cap against the biting wind, he looked back in the direction he'd travelled.

Although the sky was leaden, from this elevation he could make out the whole of Mount Bay, stretching from Longrock and St Michael's Mount, past Penzance, to the green cut of Lamorna Vale.

When he turned again, there was an owl ahead of him, swooping low over some potential quarry in the rough grass. Its great golden eyes spotted him at once, and as it flew off it gave a mischievous cackle. Tomas was sure he'd never seen or heard this bird before. He would try to remember its plumage – brown-barred, with black patches on the underside of its wings – and look it up when he got home.

Chyangwyns was an imposing stone house that looked

to Tomas more like a Georgian manor than a farmhouse. He headed for the front door and straightened his coat before ringing the bell.

The Sunday Times, wrapped in plastic, was sitting on the doormat. He picked it up just as the door was opened by a stocky woman, smartly dressed in a dark woollen trouser suit. She was in her early forties, he guessed, with dark hair severely pulled back, and she wore large black-framed glasses, which gave her eyes a penetrating stare. She took the paper from him.

'Hold on.'

She turned and went back inside.

'Four weeks, is it?' she called back to him.

He realised she thought he was the delivery boy.

'No!' he called. 'I'm Tomas Lock!'

The woman reappeared, staring at him.

'I have an appointment with Ms Mundey,' he explained, trying to sound business-like.

When she hesitated, he thought she was going to ask him to come inside. Instead, she stiffened slightly.

'You'll probably find her over at the stables.'

She gestured with a quick sideward tilt of the head. As she was about to close the door she must have seen the uncertain look on his face, because she added, 'It's round the back. Follow the path to the farm track, then left.'

She closed the door.

Tomas was confused and becoming anxious. Was Jenna Mundey out riding? Wasn't she expecting him? Had she forgotten he was coming?

The gravel path edged round the library at the side of the house. He looked in at the empty built-in bookshelves on either side of the mantelpiece. In the middle of the room were tea chests filled with books. Paint-spattered drop sheets covered the carpet.

The path made a sudden right turn and went through a tall yew hedge. On the other side was the farm track and the farmyard.

Clustered around a stone barn and granary were the dairy, cowsheds and other disused outbuildings. A new-looking black and white Mini Cooper was parked inside an open-fronted carriage house.

As he crossed the track to have a closer look, a wire-haired fox terrier came prancing toward him, giving a half-hearted barking welcome. Tomas called to it, but the dog put its nose to the ground and pretended to follow a scent that took him round behind the barn.

Looking up the track toward the edge of the moor he saw another building and headed that way.

It became obvious to Tomas, as he approached, that these were no longer working stables. Between the stables on the left and the barn on the right was an enclosed yard. The stable block itself was a single-storey stone building with tall, square rooms at either end. The middle section, where four stable doors had originally opened onto the yard, was now enclosed within a long glass conservatory that created a passageway, connecting the rooms at either end. Inside it were rows of tubs and planters holding flowering shrubs and miniature citrus trees. Jasmine and other vines climbed the conservatory walls, half obscuring the view from outside.

There were smoking chimneys at both gabled ends. The room facing the track had a bay window. Propped against the wall next to the half-glazed front door was a tile that read: *The Fogou*.

'Foo-goo?' he whispered.

Such a strange name – 'cave' in Cornish – to give to

this building. Fogous were long underground stone tunnels with side chambers, buried under mounds of earth, thousands of years old.

Tomas had explored all twelve fogous scattered around West Penwith and he had always wondered at the incredible amount of time and energy the Iron Age people must have spent constructing them – and no one knew why. Some people supposed they were places of safety.

Once, sitting inside Boleigh Fogou, its corbelled walls and its silent shadows told him that this was a place for the spirit, and that the spirit was neither masculine like Tregonebris nor feminine like Sancreed Well. He'd gone back there several times since then.

He took off his cap, knocked on the door and waited. He could see movement inside, and then the door was opened by a woman he recognised as Jenna Mundey.

She put the dustpan and brush she was holding on the floor behind the door, looking surprised or flustered or both. But when she gazed directly at him her expression softened a little.

'You must be... Tomas Lock?'

'Yes,' he said, relieved. She was expecting him after all.

'Jenna Mundey.' She gave his hand a firm shake. 'Come in.'

TWO

The room gave the illusion of being larger than it was because of its high ceiling, relatively diminutive furnishings, and the ornateness of its décor.

Jenna Mundey was wearing a green hooded top, black jodhpurs and brown boots. Her long black hair was pinned back with a silver Celtic clasp. Her face was handsome rather than beautiful, Tomas thought, with deep green eyes and a smile more welcoming and curious than at first.

'Have we met before, Tomas?'

He blushed. 'Last September, after your poetry reading in Exeter. You signed my copy of *Prismatic Vision*.'

'I remember! You were with a rather tall young man.'

'Yes, my friend Lorcan.'

'Lorcan. Such a lovely Irish name.'

'He *is* Irish – Lorcan McCall – but he calls himself Lorca.'

She raised her eyebrows. 'Brave lad.'

'He's at university there, so I stayed over with him. Otherwise it would have been too far to go.'

'Yes, it would! Let me take your things.'

He handed her his cap and tucked the folder under

his chin while he undid his coat. But as he slipped it off she took the file and tossed it onto the table by the bay window.

'Do sit. I'll just be a minute.'

She indicated a pair of armchairs set at angles to each other, facing the stove.

Tomas listened to her footsteps fading through the conservatory to the other end of the building.

He felt nervous and wished he'd managed to hold onto his folder. He did his best to flatten his curly hair over the wound, then held out his hands toward the welcoming warmth of the stove. It was a beautiful grey-green enamel range, decorated with filigree. Next to it sat a basket of logs, and above was a deep pine shelf holding canisters, pottery jars and jugs.

A door opened and closed at the other end of the stables. The smell of jasmine and orange blossom wafted through from the conservatory, its delicate scent adding an exotic dimension to the place.

The fox terrier strolled into the room, gave him a polite wag of the tail and lay down on the braided rug in front of the stove.

Either side of this stove were large oil paintings, clearly by the same artist: a blurry moorland scene, bright with heather, and a more abstract stormy seascape that included Lamorna Cove and its quay.

There was a Welsh dresser against the inner wall and, at the bay window opposite, two ladder-back chairs faced each other across a round table, empty except for his folder.

Jenna began speaking before she appeared.

'I'm surprised you and Digory didn't meet on the drive. You must have just missed each other.'

He felt his face burn.

'Oh! I'm sorry, Ms Mundey, he did... '

'Call me, Jenna,' she interrupted, going to the stove. 'And are you Tom?'

'No, Tomas, without an "h". Actually, we *did* meet – at the bottom of the drive, but – I don't know why exactly, I told him I wanted to walk the rest of the way here on my own. I'm sorry if he... '

She was staring at him, bemused. 'What are you talking about, Tomas?'

'Your husband? Digory? When I was starting up the drive he stopped and offered me a lift... '

She laughed, putting a hand over her mouth.

'Digory!' she repeated.

He was confused and embarrassed.

She lifted the stove lid and placed an enamelled kettle on the hotplate, then bent down to scratch the dog's ear.

'This is Digory, Tomas.'

'Oh, no! How stupid of me... '

He shook his head and flinched in pain, unable to join in with her laughter.

She sat in the other armchair and gazed at the logs blazing behind the glass of the fire door. Seeing her smile, he wondered if she was imagining his encounter, in one permutation or the other, with Digory.

'Who was that man, then?'

She continued staring into the fire, the brightness fading from her eyes.

'That must have been Edward.'

He could see that she wasn't going to say anything more, so he straightened himself into a more upright position.

'Thank you very much for agreeing to see me.'

She woke from her reverie.

'It's my pleasure. In fact I'm flattered. This is a "first" for me.'

'Me too.'

He immediately felt stupid for having said it.

'So, you walked here. Where have you come from?'

'Lamorna Cove.'

'Lamorna,' she repeated, drawing out the syllables in such a way that the word sounded strangely foreign to him.

'You live there?'

'Yes.'

'I have a painter friend who has a studio just up from the cove – Kitto... Christopher Quick?'

'I don't think I know him.'

There was an awkward silence.

'I love Lamorna,' she told him. 'The harbour, and that mysterious little valley. I imagine it gets very crowded with holiday makers and ramblers a lot of the time.'

'Yes, except when the weather's bad. Then it can feel sort of... empty.'

'So, you take the bus to college every day? Or do you walk to Penzance as well?'

'No, there's a bus. And I get a lift with my father sometimes. He works at the hotel near Newlyn. I was going to... '

She waited for him to continue.

'You were going to...?'

' ...to get a motorbike for my birthday. But... it's not worth it. Not now. I'll be at university before the end of the year, hopefully.'

'Are you Aquarius or Pisces?'

He was surprised by her inquisitiveness.

'Aquarius. I'll be twenty on Tuesday.'

'I'm an Aquarian as well.'

She seemed pleased to have established this link between them.

Tomas wasn't very good at telling people's age. Could she be thirty-five? More or less, he thought. But there was something youthful about her that didn't have anything to do with age.

'Do you mind my asking why you're just doing your A levels now, at twenty, Tomas?'

He did mind, and he struggled not to let himself become distracted by a barrage of uncomfortable memories.

'I took a year off, that's all.' He hoped she wasn't going to pursue the matter.

'I see... so, how did your class decide which one of you would be doing this interview?'

He blushed. 'There wasn't much discussion about it. They all said it should be me, since it was my idea. Everyone contributed questions, though.'

He glanced over at the folder on the table, then remembered that the sheet of questions was no longer inside.

'Shall we get started? We can sit here by the window.'

He grabbed the folder before sitting opposite her.

'Ready when you are, Tomas.'

THREE

The atmosphere became more formal as he opened the folder, took out his pen and a blank sheet of paper and arranged them neatly in front of him. When he looked up she was giving him an indulgent smile.

'First of all,' he said, awkwardly, 'since it's your *Selected Verses* in our A level syllabus, we thought I shouldn't ask you about your other books.'

'Okay, that's fair enough.'

'But... I suppose you'll have to update *Selected Verses* sooner or later, since it was published... four years ago? Then *Prismatic Vision* about two years ago? And *Bimarian Ground* last September.'

She sat back. 'That's right.'

'So you must be writing poems all the time.'

'Well, not *all* the time.'

'No, I didn't mean... '

'I think I know what you mean, Tomas. But, is there a question in all this?'

He flushed, getting into a muddle already, wishing again that he had that sheet of questions.

'Did you decide which poems would go into *Selected Verses*? Was anybody else involved?'

'Ah. You mean, who selected?'

'Something like that.'

'I could say it was just me – my decisions – since I had the last word on every one of them. But to be fair, my editor Pam was a great help. It's a bit like choosing your favourite poets I suppose. I could never have been objective enough to do it on my own. Together we managed it without too much bickering.'

Tomas made a note, then asked, 'Who *are* your favourite poets?'

She narrowed her eyes, looked out through the window, then back at him.

'I don't actually have any favourites. Sorry.'

He realised that he was just letting his mind wander wherever it pleased! What were the questions he *should* be asking?

'At Exeter you read other people's poems as well as your own. I was surprised – so was Lorca.'

'The programme was called, *A Poetry Reading with Jenna Mundey*, wasn't it?'

'Yes, but you could easily have spent the whole evening reading just your own verse. I think that's what people expected.'

She looked concerned. 'Were you disappointed?'

'Oh, no, not at all!' he protested, feeling more sick and stupid. 'I didn't mean that. It's just that... well, why didn't you?'

'There are so many thousands of gifted poets Tomas – and thousands of incredible poems in every language. But most people don't come across more than a handful in a lifetime.'

'No.'

'When I prepare a reading it's usually a shared event

with one or two other poets. It wasn't like that at Exeter, and I thought it would be a bit egotistical of me to read just my own verse.'

The water in the kettle had begun to simmer. She got up, closed the stove lid and placed the kettle on top.

'When I'm planning a reading I always remind myself that people are going to be there because they love poetry, not just because it's Jenna Mundey.'

He wondered whether this was true. Would he have made such an effort to go all that way if he'd known she would be reading other poets as well? Yes, of course he would. He remembered the excitement he'd felt that whole evening.

'You read them so beautifully. It was like a recital – as though you knew all those poems by heart. It made me want to find them in the library and read them again.'

'Good, I'm glad. Actually I have memorised lots of poems. I love hearing them spoken.'

'Sometimes I *have* to read a poem aloud before I can understand it.' Then he added, 'Not your poems, though.'

She grinned. 'Reading poetry aloud should be a celebration of life – of simply being alive.'

He hoped he would never forget her saying this to him. He looked down at the almost blank sheet of paper, wondering what else he could ask that might draw out another such response.

'What did it feel like having *Prismatic Vision* short-listed for the Whitbread Prize?'

She brushed back a strand of hair.

'It was wonderful, of course. Very good news for me and for Moon Press.'

Her reply pulled his muddled mind in another direction.

'Aren't you ever tempted to move to a bigger publisher?

In one newspaper interview you said that poetry needs to reach as wide an audience as it can find.'

'Yes, I believe that – very deeply. There's a poem by William Carlos Williams called "Asphodel, That Greeny Flower". In it he says:

> *It is difficult*
> *to get the news from poems*
> *yet men die miserably every day*
> *for lack*
> *of what is found there.*

And it's true.'

'Yes.'

He jotted down the lines. He would have to study them later – try to make sense of them. For now he had to concentrate harder on what he was supposed to be doing.

'Anyway, I'll always want The Moon,' she said, more to herself than to him.

Another question that he knew wasn't on the list sprang into his mind. He was considering asking it when he realised that she was asking him a question.

'Have you read *all* my books, Tomas?'

He squirmed.

'I think so. We don't have to read them all. I just... I like them very much.'

'So, do *you* have a favourite?'

'*Bimarian Ground*,' he replied without hesitation. 'I think it's brilliant!'

'Not just because it's the latest, I hope.'

'No! There are lots of things I'd like to ask you about it... '

'Go on, then.'

'... but it's not in the syllabus. It wouldn't be fair to the rest of the class.'

Jenna glanced around the room and gave him a mischievous look.

'They're not here, are they?'

'No.'

'Go on, then,' she repeated.

He couldn't believe his luck. But should he be doing this?

'*Bimarian* means two seas?'

'That's right. I found the word in an old English dictionary and liked the sound of it. *Bimarian Ground* is the land between two seas. In fact, it's right here – midway between the English Channel and the Celtic Sea.'

He scribbled '*½ way*' onto the page.

'I was hoping to find a Cornish place name for the title, but didn't manage it.'

He looked up. 'If you lived at Lamorna you could have used *Lamorna*. In Cornish it means *A place by the sea*.'

'Yes, it's a beautiful word – *and* it would have been lipogramatic.'

Her saying this prompted him to ask the question he most wanted answered.

'What made you decide to write a whole book in lipograms?'

She scrutinised her folded hands and said nothing. It was as though no one had ever asked her that question before. But that couldn't be true. Maybe she just never told anyone. He shouldn't have asked.

'I suppose you could say that I was having trouble with my "e"s at the time.'

He stared at her, puzzled.

'But there aren't any "e"s in the whole book. I mean,

that's what you did – not use any words with "e"s in them...'

'Sorry, Tomas, I'm joking.'

For a moment she seemed so preoccupied he was sure she wasn't going to give him a direct answer.

'At the time, I felt I *had* to write those poems, or something like them, but I couldn't do it.'

She paused.

'After a few false starts, I realised that what I needed was a form that would impose as much constraint on me as I could bear. Some contrivance that would be so limiting it would force me to concentrate on just the process of writing.'

'You mean, always having to keep in mind what the poem has to do? The way you have to decide its shape – how many lines, the meter, the rhyme scheme?'

'Yes, that's right. But *you* don't decide, do you? *It* decides.'

He felt a jolt in his stomach, then at the back of his head. What was she saying? *It?* If he didn't concentrate harder she'd lose him. She *was* losing him!

'Like with haiku. It's such a simple form: five, then seven, then five syllables. You can't begin to write a haiku without keeping those rules in mind, can you?'

'No.'

'Recently I've been experimenting with some Welsh verse forms called *englynion*. There are eight variations in all, some more complex than others... '

What was she talking about? He was struggling, getting more confused.

'I've been writing *englyn unodl union*, which has thirty syllables: four lines – ten, six, seven, and then seven syllables, all using the same rhyme. In the first line the rhyme is introduced somewhere after the sixth syllable.

Then it recurs at the end of the other three lines. Are you with me?'

He started to shake his head, stopped and wrote on the paper: *4 lines = 10,6,7,7.* He began thinking he was back in English class.

'Every constraint – like those Welsh ones, and the lipogram – every binding rule in poetry is there to serve a purpose. Which is, ultimately, to give you freedom.'

He stared at her, trying to make sense of this contradiction.

'I don't understand. Rules – any kind of rules – are there to restrict you, aren't they?'

'No, not really. Do you play football, Tomas?'

He shook his head and winced, but she didn't seem to notice.

'I've always loved watching the game: the grace and precision, the amazing athleticism of the players. None of it would be possible without strictly agreed rules and rigid boundaries marking out the pitch, would it?'

'No,' he murmured.

'But playing by those rules, within those boundaries, letting them work for you... well, it's beautiful. It gives the players such creative freedom.'

'I think I understand.'

'The lipogram was just the constraint I needed. It enabled me to *play* again.'

The idea that playing could be a part of writing poetry seemed strange to Tomas, but he didn't say so.

'At the time, I didn't think I'd ever be able to write another poem. So it was rather bloody-minded of me to try to write even *one* poem without any "e"s!'

'It's such an unusual thing to do.'

'But as soon as I got started, really committed myself

to comply with the constraint, I discovered that I *had* to think creatively. It was an incredible process. I could use the lipogram's one simple rule, to leave out a vowel – in my case the letter "e" – and keeping to that rule gave me amazing freedom. I could let the poem find its own voice. I was more than just compliant, I became completely absorbed in it.'

'How could it do that?'

Tomas hoped she would give a simple explanation, and wished that she wouldn't speak so fast.

'"E" is the most common letter in the English language, so it's difficult to avoid it, but I discovered ways around it as I went along.'

If only he wasn't feeling so ill, getting so confused! He was sure that what she was telling him now was more important than anything he might ever learn about writing poetry. He wanted to remember it, like what she had said earlier about... something about... being alive. What was it?

'I found that by changing the past tense of a verb into the present tense – by adding "ing" – you lose a lot of "e"s.'

Tomas wanted to shout, 'Stop!' She was losing him.

'For instance,' she went on, '*doing*, not done. *Living*, not lived. *Loving*, not loved. And using the active rather than the passive voice keeps you in the moment. Do you see?'

He didn't. Not most of it. Not now.

'You can't use *he* or *she* or *me* or *we* – or *they* or *them*. But, *you* brings the other person directly into the poem. So does *us* and *our*. It all makes the poem more immediate, more intimate.'

Feeling much weaker, he couldn't make an intelligent comment.

'I like them very much.'

'Thank you Tomas, so do I. Most of them, anyway.'

She lifted the stove lid and put the kettle back onto the hotplate.

'I'll make some tea.'

When she'd left the room he looked down at his few notes, which didn't make any sense to him now. This wasn't how he'd imagined it would be. This was much more... he couldn't think of the word. His head was pounding.

Hearing the faint clatter of crockery, he decided that if there was a kitchen there was bound to be a toilet in the stables as well. And maybe somewhere to lie down if he felt he was going to...

She came in carrying a tea tray and placed it on the side table between the armchairs.

'Another question?' she asked.

He didn't know what she meant by 'another question'.

He looked into her eyes. For a split second he wasn't sure who she was or what he was doing there.

'Tomas?'

He pretended to read from his notes.

'What are you writing now?'

'Something quite different. A long poem of triads, to illustrate a prose work called *The Sacred Cauldron*. It's come from my interest in the Welsh sagas. Do you know *The Mabinogion*?'

'No.'

'The number three plays an important role all the way through them: the triads.'

He wrote the number *3* on the paper.

'In the tale of Culhwch and Olwen, only three men escape alive from the Battle of Camlan, and I decided to write three poems about them, one for each. The first for Sandde Bryd Angel, who survived the battle unharmed because he was so beautiful. Everyone on the battlefield thought he must be their ministering angel!'

'You wrote a poem – "Ministering Angel" – in *Prismatic Vision*.'

'Yes, but I re-wrote it after... a friend and I went our separate ways.'

He shut his eyes and half-whispered:

> *'Dearest angel face,*
> *always looking out*
> *toward the farthest, faintest edge.*
> *No one*
> *could ever hold him back*
> *or hold him long;*
> *not ever in one place*
> *and never close enough.'*

When he opened his eyes he saw that she was studying him.

'Tomas?'

His face burned and his head throbbed. How could she not notice how ill he was feeling?

'Another question?' she asked.

'Is there a toilet here I could use?'

'Yes, of course.'

FOUR

Tomas and Digory followed Jenna through the conservatory to the far end of the stable block.

A room the same size as the one they'd left had been partitioned. There was a good-sized kitchen with a long slate work surface, wooden cupboards and drawers, a larder by the kitchen door, and a green Rayburn against the back wall. Everything looked newly fitted.

The bathroom, reached through a lobby, included a toilet, a shower and a pottery washbasin resting on a wooden shelf. Hand towels hung on the radiator under a small window that looked out onto a low walled garden, recently planted with rectangles of box hedges and herbs. Beyond it stretched the moor and a blackening sky.

Inexplicably this prospect reminded Tomas so forcefully of the Circle Garden at Penmount Crematorium that he quickly turned away.

He sat on the toilet lid fighting back tears. The headache and dizziness were becoming unbearable.

What's happening? What is happening to me?

After washing his face he put a cupped hand over the lump on the back of his head, still hot and raw. He saw himself in the mirror and was shocked by how pale and haggard he looked.

Jenna was filling a milk jug. He leaned against the back door, looking around the kitchen.

'What was this room before?'

'It was the tack room.'

'Do you... live here?' he asked curiously.

She placed a bowl of sugar and a jar of honey on the tray with the milk. 'Yes, I do.'

'When that... ' He started over. 'When the lady at the house told me I'd find you at the stables I thought she meant you'd been out riding.'

'That was my sister, Ester,' Jenna said, picking up the tray, then putting it down again. 'Yes, I've always loved riding. But I've lost my horse. Ebril.'

'I'm sorry.'

He wished he hadn't mentioned it.

'I haven't been here very long. The Fogou itself hasn't been here long either.'

He wanted to know more, know everything about this place and the woman who lived here. But all he could manage to say was, 'It hasn't?'

She leaned back on the counter and, to his surprise, began to tell him.

'My husband Edward gave up farming after the foot and mouth epidemic. There were grants available for diversification, and last year he decided to turn the farm buildings into self-catering holiday cottages, starting with the stables.

'Without Ebril I knew I'd never ride again, so when most of the building work was done I began coming over here – doing the planting in the conservatory, laying out the new garden at the back. Eventually I started using the hay store, which is now the sitting room, as my study. Would you like to see?'

'Yes.'

She led him to the first stable door along the passageway and opened it.

'This is the bedroom,' she told him.

It was a cell-like room, with whitewashed walls and a wooden floor, bare except for another small braided rug. The single bed was covered with a patchwork quilt. There was a bedside table and lamp, a chest of drawers and a captain's chest beside the radiator. As in the other rooms, the wall between this stable and the next was only six feet high, with a metal partition grill above. Each of the stables had a skylight set into the pitched roof.

Opening the second door she said, 'This is where I study'.

The room was a miniature library, with half-filled bookcases and shelves around three walls. A writing table stood in the middle, a captain's chair tucked under it, and an oil lamp sitting on top. In the corner by the radiator was a tea chest full of books.

Tomas thought he might be on a guided tour in a little museum, being conducted through it by the curator herself.

'Finally,' she said, opening the third door, 'this is where I can occupy myself with other things.'

Unlike the first two, this little room was carpeted. A guitar was propped against a stool in one corner; a sound system and CDs lined a long shelf above a pine table and bench. Two oversized cushions lay on the floor.

Tomas felt certain there was a fourth stable. Turning from the doorway, he saw the door, glanced back at Jenna for permission, then opened it.

He stared into the strange, surreal space: a loose box, with wooden kick panels covering the lower half of the walls, a hanging manger in one corner, and a rug rail. But this wasn't only a stable, because beside a pine box was a folded futon mattress, and on the whitewashed back wall was a verse written in fine black script:

> *And in this holy hour a fuming rain*
> *Might swallow up my midnight and my pain.*

These were the last lines of 'April', one of his favourite sonnets in *Bimarian Ground*.

She stood in the doorway.

'This was Ebril's stable. I couldn't decide what to do with it. I have all the space I need for myself, so I've left it for now.'

Tomas managed a careful nod.

She went to the kitchen to fetch the tray. Left on his own, he went back to the sitting room.

To his amazement, it was beginning to snow. Large, flat flakes were blowing against the bay window and eddying around in the yard.

'We can carry on over here, if you like.' She set the tray on the side table.

Digory trotted through from the kitchen and scratched at the door.

'He loves the snow.'

She let him out, then lifted a canister from the shelf above the stove, spooned tea into the pot and filled it with boiling water.

'I haven't answered all your questions, have I?'

Questions? He hadn't asked any of his classmates' questions! Had he? He couldn't remember. He leaned back, wanting to close his eyes, then sat forward again.

'It doesn't really matter.'

She looked puzzled. 'Doesn't it?'

He wondered if it did. 'Should I ask a few more?'

'Only if you want to.'

Was there a curtness in her reply? He sighed.

'I don't think I can... What do you want to do?'

She lifted a large heart-shaped wooden box down from the shelf and held it open for him. He looked inside, took out one of the spicy sugar biscuits and began removing its fine tissue wrapping.

'Take more. It's Valentine's Day.'

He took another two, wondering if he'd eaten anything at all today. He couldn't remember.

They sat in silence with their tea and biscuits.

Then she asked, 'Do you write poetry, Tomas?'

'Yes.'

'What do you write about?'

'Well... anything, really.'

He knew he couldn't discuss his poetry with her at this moment.

She gave him a few seconds to consider.

'I mean your subject matter, your bug-bears.'

'I suppose I write about... feelings mostly.'

'Good. And what do they look like?'

He rubbed his forehead.

'My feelings?'

'I meant your poems. But your feelings, if you prefer.'

'No!'

His hands were trembling and he nearly dropped the teacup as he put it down on the table. Another wave of anxiety and confusion, this time triggered by the thought of having to turn his feelings into images, broke over him.

She remained silent, so he'd have to say something.

'Lately I've been writing sonnets. I like the form a lot.'

'So do I. Which brings us back to constraints, doesn't it. Lipograms, sonnets, sestinas, villanelles. Wonderful devices.'

He stared at her. 'Have you ever been a teacher?'

She suppressed a laugh. 'No, I have not! Whatever made you ask me that?'

'I don't know. At secondary school, and now at college, so much of it's boring. Even English. We spend so much time analysing literature and not much time bringing the words to life – celebrating. You'd make a good teacher, the way you... '

The pounding on the door made them both jump.

Jenna got to her feet. 'Excuse me a minute.'

The man's face was red and he looked very angry.

'Is he with *you* or with *me*?' he shouted in a hoarse voice.

Tomas stood up, his heart pounding. The man sounded like his father – even looked like him. How could he have found him here?

'I said, is he with you or with me?' He leaned close to Jenna's face. '*You* decide!'

She took a step back and held up her hand.

They were arguing about him – about something he had done! But what was it? What had he done? He couldn't remember.

'Please, just tell me what you want. As you can see, I'm... '

'You're doing this deliberately, aren't you?' he sputtered.

Who was this man? He looked and sounded the way his father sometimes did. Then... could she be his mother? Did she need his protection?

As he took a step toward them, a wave of nausea welled up. God, he was going to be sick!

Hearing Tomas approach she went outside, signalling for the man to follow. With the door closed, he could barely hear them.

'What *is* it? What's *happened*?' she was asking in a loud voice, now becoming fainter.

Straining to hear, Tomas steadied himself, holding onto the back of the chair, then staggered to the door.

They were in the yard somewhere, but he couldn't see them. Huge flakes of snow were swirling around, ticking against the glass.

He felt numb.

The odd snatches of conversation he could hear made no sense. Now she was shouting, insistent.

'What are you... Tie him up! Where...'

He should go to her and stop this from happening.

He opened the door. The snow blew into his eyes on a cuff of wind, taking his breath away.

When he realised that he was going to faint he slammed the door. The room was spinning.

FIVE

'I've had just about enough of this, Jenna!'

Edward was still blustering.

She blinked against the sharp snowflakes and pulled up her hood, feeling a reflex she'd become familiar with recently – that shift from placating wife to angry separate woman – and she didn't want to control it. 'Enough of what, for God's sake?'

She continued staring at him and wouldn't look away until he lowered his eyes.

'I was painting in the library – propped the doors open to let out the fumes – and in he comes, trailing mud and wiping himself against the wall. I could have killed him!'

She headed toward Chyangwyns, looking straight ahead. 'Where is he now?'

'I told you. I've tied him in the barn.' There was less anger in his voice. 'Either keep him inside with you, or go with him when he has to go out. At least until he gets used to this... circus!'

He stopped, but she walked on. 'If you're still sure you want him with you.'

She struggled to open the barn door, which was sagging on its rusted hinges, but refused to let Edward help her.

Digory was tied to a pallet with a length of baling twine. She released him, then swung round to face Edward. She had to wait until she felt calm enough to speak.

'Please give this a fair trial, Edward – a few more days. I'll try to remember. It's just that, with my visitor I'd forgotten... '

'Who is that boy, anyway?'

'He's come to interview me, from the college.'

'A rude little bugger, if you ask me.'

She felt her anger return.

'I'm sure he thinks the same about you! Your manners today are... '

Edward strode out of the barn. She took a step forward, shouting after him.

'Your behaviour's becoming absurd and offensive! Did you forget to take your medication this morning?'

He stopped.

'No, probably not – not with Ester in charge.'

She and Digory waited until he was out of sight; stood listening to a pair of pigeons high on a beam above them.

'Come on, Digs.'

She pushed the barn door closed, gave it a hard kick, then headed back to The Fogou.

Edward was impossible on days like this. A year or two ago he would have saved his rancour for the fox that managed to get into the hen run, or the latest edict from Defra regarding hedge-trimming or listeria in unpasturised milk products. Nowadays he seemed to hone in on more vulnerable targets. She'd become used to being one of them, but raging against Digory and her young visitor was pathetic.

She turned the doorknob and pushed, but the sitting room door wouldn't open. She tried again, brushing snow from the glass and peering inside. Digory whined, then barked.

'Tomas?' she called, giving the door a final push. It opened just far enough for her to see the sole of his trainer.

She raced to the kitchen door, Digory beside her, and grabbed her mobile from the counter.

Then she rushed through the conservatory and knelt over Tomas' crumpled body, lying against the door.

'Tomas?'

When he didn't move she touched his hand, which was white and cold.

'Tomas!'

Reaching round to feel his forehead, she saw the swollen gash, half hidden in a bloody mat of curls at the back of his head.

'Oh my God!'

She felt for a pulse at his wrist and pressed the speed-dial button on the phone.

'Ester, come to The Fogou! The boy's unconscious! I don't know what's wrong with him! Come through the kitchen door. Please hurry!'

She bent over him, resting an arm on his shoulder.

'What's happened?' she whispered to him.

When Digory began whining again, she pushed him back.

'Go lie down, Digory! Go on!'

Looking at Tomas' face, now peaceful and expression-less, she realised how strained and uncomfortable he'd been over the past hour.

Ester was speaking as she rushed in.

'Let me see him.'

Jenna moved aside to give her sister space, watching as

she methodically checked his vital signs, lifting his eyelids to assess his condition.

'Look at the wound on the back of his head.'

Ester parted the hair and had a cursory look.

'How long has he been like this?'

'I was only gone ten minutes. He was fine when I left.'

Ester gave her a doubtful glance.

'Honestly! He was okay when Edward arrived.'

Under Ester's instructions, they half lifted, half slid Tomas over onto the rug in front of the stove and eased him into the recovery position.

'Are you going to call for an ambulance?' Ester asked.

'Should I?' She reached for the phone.

'No, wait. Let's see if Arthur's home first. If he is he might come over.' Ester grabbed the phone and dialled the doctor's number from memory.

Please! Jenna whispered to whatever holy presence might be listening. *Please let him be all right.*

The snow had stopped falling just before dusk, leaving a grey covering that made the drive a slippery mash. The sky was still heavy and the air damp. Where the farm track met the drive, Jenna stood shivering and impatient, looking down in the direction of St Just.

Headlights finally appeared on the straight stretch of the lane. The car raced along and then slowed down for the turning into the drive. A minute later Dr Sanders' Volvo was speeding toward her, splashing slush and spray onto the verges. She waved both arms, directing him onto the farm track, and then followed behind.

When she caught up he was at the front door, bag in hand, wearing a skiing jacket and jeans. He knocked once and went in.

Jenna paused for a moment. Arthur looked stockier and greyer than when she'd last seen him – probably at some event at the Minerva Centre, where he was a consultant to Ester and her volunteers. As she opened the door she found the doctor kneeling over the boy, examining him just as Ester had done half an hour before. They were speaking in low voices – a professional pair, completely in command of the situation.

Jenna felt relieved enough to sit at the table and close her eyes.

Almost at once, chaos erupted. Tomas began moaning, and then screaming, thrashing about so wildly that Jenna thought he was having a seizure.

Arthur and Ester leaned back to give him room, watching like detached observers, until Arthur laid his hands on the boy's shoulders in a gesture of comfort and gentle restraint. The effect of this contact was sudden and violent. Tomas shouted, hitting out and managing to kick Arthur in the small of his back.

Ester grabbed his ankles and held them down. She mouthed a question to the doctor, and he nodded. When he had stopped struggling, she pulled off his trainers and, in a calm but commanding voice, called out his name.

Tomas' eyes were still closed, but Jenna saw a look come over his face that suggested he was conscious now. Ester caught her eye and shook her head – a gesture that seemed judgemental of her rather than the boy.

Tomas opened his eyes and immediately closed them again. A deep moaning in his chest culminated in an explosion of vomit.

Jenna gasped and stood up, pressing her hands to her breast.

'Get a towel – and some water,' Ester commanded without looking up.

When she reached the relative quiet of the kitchen, Jenna didn't want to go back, but of course she had no choice. Instead she distanced herself from what was actually happening in there by simply giving her full attention to what she'd been instructed to do. She managed, for a minute or two, to avoid thinking about the reason why she was doing it. It was a way of detaching herself, an emotional constraint she had learnt when her mother died.

She took a basin from under the sink and concentrated on half filling it with equal amounts of hot and cold water, since neither had been specified. Then she took her towel and flannel from the bathroom rail without thinking about what use they were going to be put to.

When she returned to the sitting room and saw Tomas retching and Arthur supporting his head and neck, she wanted to escape again. Her head was a jumble of thoughts and feelings, and she began to feel sick and faint herself. But having done one errand for them, she might be required to do another, so she couldn't leave. She sat by the window, peering out into the comforting darkness.

Tomas was making rasping, panting noises and moans – coughing and stifling cries. She could make out odd words and phrases spoken in a delirium by a voice she hardly recognised. He was like a pathetic child – a whimpering, whinging infant left alone too long.

How could this be happening?

She scanned her mind for an explanation, or for someone to blame. Edward, of course, for his outburst an hour ago – barging in here and upsetting everything. Herself as well. She'd been blathering on about her poetry, not noticing or even suspecting that something was seriously wrong with the boy. And Tomas himself, who obviously knew he was injured. He must have felt unwell, but said nothing – done nothing to alert her or to help himself.

Now he was murmuring gibberish, making no sense at all. It sounded like heyjyk, and then lorkee. Heyjyk... lorkee. Speaking in tongues?

There was a poem about a mad boy – or was it a child possessed? She couldn't remember who wrote it. Maybe one day she would calmly recollect this bizarre scene, capture it in words, entitle the poem Epiphany, or...

She stopped herself, mortified. How could she be thinking such a thing at such a moment? Whatever had drawn her there?

She knew it was fear – trying to control her fear and uncertainty. It was another ploy she'd used when her mother died.

'Are you going to phone for an ambulance?' Ester asked the doctor. Before he could reply, Tomas screamed, 'No!' – a long, wailing cry – twisting and contorting his limbs as they tried to restrain him.

Jenna had had enough.

'Tomas!'

She jumped up and went over to him.

'Stop it, Tomas! That's enough! Now just stop it!'

And he did stop. Immediately.

She continued to stand over him, hands on hips, until she saw the tension in his body begin to dissipate. In another minute he was breathing more naturally, falling asleep.

When she noticed Ester and Arthur staring at her she gave them back a look both surprised and defiant.

Now there were four of them in her sitting room.

Dr Sanders sat at the table writing up his notes, using Tomas' pen and a sheet of paper he'd taken from the folder. Ester sat beside him, watching. Jenna and Edward were sitting in front of the stove, with Digory lying between them. Edward was concerned and sympathetic when Ester told him what had happened. Jenna glanced critically at him as he stubbed out his cigarette in a little pottery dish on the side table.

She was disconcerted – her personal space was much too crowded – and she wanted them just to finish and go.

'I was pretty sure it was PCS as soon as I saw him,' Ester told Arthur.

'PCS?' Edward asked.

'Sorry – post-concussive syndrome.'

'We can't be certain of that,' Arthur said, still writing. 'Not without seeing the images.'

'It could be PTSS, you mean.'

'Let's not speculate, Ester.'

'Will they do a CAT?'

'No, I've asked for an MRI.' He looked over at Edward and Jenna. 'That's the Magnetic Resonance Imaging scan radiology will be doing in the morning.'

Edward nodded.

'It's more sensitive than a CAT scan.'

He continued writing, and then looked at Jenna. 'A relative or friend could accompany Tomas into the scanning room, if he agrees. There's no radiation involved, just a lot of noise.'

'I see,' she said, thoughtfully. 'What did Mr Lock have to say about the injury?'

'He said he didn't know anything about it. Seemed surprised at first, but not overly concerned.'

Ester made a critical huffing sound. 'He would say that if he'd been abusing the boy.' She glanced at her sister. 'How'd you know he worked at that hotel, Jen?'

'Tomas told me.'

The room was silent for a moment.

'I tried to put him off,' she said to no one in particular. 'I thought I had, until he turned up.'

'Who?' Edward asked.

'Tomas, of course! I wanted to postpone the interview until I felt more settled. But I couldn't contact the college because it's Sunday. By the time I'd trawled through all the Locks in the phone book and left a message he must have been on his way here. I'd completely forgotten he was coming until this morning.'

'That's not like you, Jen.' He sounded concerned.

'I lost my diary during the move. I'm completely at sea without it!'

'We'll have a scout around,' he said, looking at Ester, who nodded.

Jenna felt she had to ask: 'Did you remember to close up the hens?'

'Yes,' he replied, in an emphatic tone that told her she needn't have asked.

'I heard a fox in the yard last night. I couldn't get back to sleep for the longest time, worrying.'

'Well, don't! There's no need.'

Arthur put the pen back into Tomas' folder and stood up.

'I'd better go and make the arrangements.'

He took off his glasses and slid them into their case. Jenna went to him.

'Thank you so much, Arthur.'

'Yes indeed,' added Ester.

He shrugged modestly. 'You were absolutely right to phone me.'

Edward opened the door for him. 'We'll see you to the car. Come on, Digs!'

He gave Jenna a peck on the cheek and they were gone. She slumped back into her chair.

Ester picked up a black bin liner and went to the door.

'Give me a call if you need anything, Jen.'

'Thanks Ester.'

'I mean it.'

Please just go!

'I know you do.'

'Goodnight.'

She continued to sit, gazing into the fire, feeling numb but not sleepy. It was weariness, mixed with disbelief at everything that had happened.

She lit the two fat candles on the dresser and switched off the lamp by the table. Then she threw the cigarette ends into the Rayburn. She leaned her elbows on the kitchen counter and bowed her head, listening to the silence and trying to clear her mind. If today was a presage of what might come to her here at The Fogou, rather than a single crazy incident, it wasn't fair. This was her place – a hard-won place of her own, damn it! Her place between two seas...

Between two stools? Between a rock and a hard place? Christ, she hoped not.

SIX

By midnight a milder, westerly breeze was blowing in off the Celtic Sea.

Jenna had filled the stove with logs and got ready for bed. She stood studying her library shelves before lifting down two books of poems by Denise Levertov. She'd recently agreed to contribute an essay to a Welsh literary quarterly about this half-Welsh poet, and the deadline was looming.

In her candle-lit bedroom she tugged on one of the long woollen pull-cords to open the skylight a crack, then sat on the low stool next to the bed. She opened one of the books and read several early poems. She re-read 'The Dreamers'. It seemed to resonate with this moment:

> *The sleeping sensual head*
> *lies nearer than her hand,*
> *but secret and remote,*
> *an impenetrable land...*
>
> *She hears the sound of midnight*
> *that breaks like a sea,*

and leans above the sleeper
as secretive as he.

She glanced over at Tomas, asleep in her bed. He was lying on his right side, in a foetal position. A heavy bandage covered the top and back of his head. He was wearing a white flannel nightshirt Edward had provided. Ester told her she'd return Tomas' clothes and her towel, washed and dried, in the morning.

She sighed and picked up the other book, turned its pages, browsing, until she came to 'The Wedding Ring':

My wedding-ring lies in a basket
as if at the bottom of a well.
Nothing will come to fish it back up
and onto my finger again.
It lies
among keys to abandoned houses,
nails waiting to be needed and hammered
into some wall,
telephone numbers with no names attached...

If she had lost her wedding ring instead of her diary, today would have turned out differently. She wouldn't have minded losing it all that much. When she'd taken it off last week she'd felt as burdened by it as she had while it was still on her finger. A few days later she'd slipped it under a pile of handkerchiefs in the bottom of her chest of drawers and had completely forgotten about it until now.

Tonight Edward had again been thoughtful and solicitous, persuading her to let Digory stay over at the house for the night. He'd even offered to sit up with her, or keep watch himself, once Arthur had decided that Tomas did not have to go into hospital if someone would keep a close eye on him overnight. But that would have meant Edward staying at The Fogou, or else moving Tomas to the house – neither of which she'd wanted.

Predictably, Ester had been inspired by the emergency. It was a pity she'd dropped out of medical school. Such a waste.

She remembered the time they'd been walking along the coastal path near Pendeen after a meal for their father's birthday. They stopped to watch a pair of seals basking on the rocks below, and she'd asked Ester why she hadn't gone on with her training – opting for nursing instead. Her cryptic reply was that her life had got in the way too much.

There was a shrill scream out in the yard. Jenna dropped the book and jumped to her feet. The vixen's almost human cry – like a deranged infant – was immediately followed by the *yark-yark-yark* of a dog fox out on the moor.

She stood there, trembling, until she felt calm enough to sit again. Then she wondered whether Edward had remembered to close up the hens before she'd asked him about it. Probably. She should try to let go of these worries; these things were no longer really her concern.

Her eyes were tired now. She closed them, feeling a heaviness creeping through every limb. She should go and make up the bed in the stable room while she still had the energy. But the silence in the room, made deeper by the now distant calling of the fox, felt reassuring.

One of the tiny candle wicks floating in the dish of oily water on the bedside table began to sputter. She opened a bottle of lavender and rosemary oil, poured some onto the water and watched as the flames grew brighter.

She didn't feel like reading, but wasn't ready to sleep either. She put the book on the floor and sat watching Tomas sleeping instead.

Such an incredible turn around in one afternoon. This ordinary teenage boy arrived here to interview her. An hour later he was comatose, delirious, hysterical – refusing to be taken to hospital or to return home.

From something Arthur had said, she assumed that his mother was dead. Was that the reason for his gap year before college?

How ironic that on this of all weekends, which she'd looked forward to spending idly here alone with Digory – sorting out her library and maybe doing some writing – someone virtually unknown to her until today was sleeping in her bed. If only she'd managed to cancel their meeting!

Now it was the tawny owl calling, distracting her from her thoughts.

Kee-wick!

Not near, probably out in the little copse.

She went to the kitchen. When the kettle had boiled, she made herself a cup of vervain tea and took it through to the sitting room. The candles on the dresser gave a soft, gentle light.

She resisted the urge to get out her notebook and begin writing. It had become a habit over the last few nights: after midnight, needing to switch off but unable to do so. If she succumbed, the results would invariably disappoint her in the morning. Tomas' folder still lay on the table. She reached inside and pulled out... a daffodil. It was crushed and wilted, but she held it to her nose. Its faint scent was odd, unfamiliar, disconsolate, if such a thing were possible.

She laid it on the table and took out the two sheets of paper. On one he'd written notes during their interview – just the quote from William Carlos Williams and a line of numbers. On the other sheet, which was wrinkled and creased, were two long lines, crooked and carelessly written. She read them, then whispered them aloud:

> *You watch, dumb, as your past slinks forward*
> * to find you.*
> *Nothing can stop this chopping of blood*
> * knots that bind you.*

Jenna found the verse disturbing, resonating with something she couldn't quite identify – like the smell of the daffodil.

Now she felt guilty, prying into Tomas' personal writing – if it was his. She should put it back into the folder. But she didn't.

They were strong, confident lines that knew what they were doing. There was a mysterious finality – almost a fatality – about them. Dirge-like, elegiac, this could be the final couplet of a sonnet. The curious cadence worked well, making it processional. That pause in the first line – the caesura – stopped you cold, anticipating the passive 'witness' of the second line, so full of assonance.

Jenna stopped herself when she realised what she was doing. Here it was again, this unattractive aspect of herself – the wretched intellectualising, the processing of experience. She put the sheets of paper and the daffodil back inside the folder and sipped her tea.

Tomas had asked if she'd been a teacher. Perhaps he'd

meant it as a compliment, because he hadn't spotted that didactic defence she sometimes used to detach herself from her emotions.

She glanced up at the two paintings, thinking about the artist, Kitto, and her willingness – her eagerness – to become emotionally and physically absorbed in this younger man. He was beautiful, like a rainbow arching over her disused life, touching her emotions. She'd abandoned her usual defensive gambit of retreating back into the shade of detachment and reason and had reached out for him.

But the aftermath – all the flotsam and jetsam she still found herself unexpectedly bumping up against in her day-to-day, plodding life – had been painful.

Her tea had gone cold, but she still sat, considering that loose hinge to her heart and beginning to shape a poem in her mind.

There was a sudden cry. At first she mistook it for the fox, but it was immediately followed by a shattering crash.

She jumped up and ran to the bedroom, now in darkness, realising at once what had happened.

'It's all right, Tomas.'

She spoke calmly, reaching for the foot of the bed.

'Just a second. I'm turning on the lamp.'

When she had, she saw that he was sitting up in bed, blinking, dazzled by the sudden brightness.

They looked down at the broken pottery bowl, the wicks and oily water spilt over the floor. He made a whimpering sound.

'It doesn't matter.'

She would leave it there for now.

'Are you all right?'

She sat on the edge of the bed, resting a hand on his

arm. He didn't move, either to relax the tension he was holding or to withdraw from her touch. But he was staring at her as though he didn't know who she was or where he was. This look frightened her.

'Do you want to use the toilet?'

He began to shake his head, cringed and cried out, then gazed around the room.

'Something to drink? A glass of water?'

He slumped down under the quilt, looking up at the skylight.

'Are you warm enough? I can close it.'

He didn't respond. She decided not to say anything more.

He closed his eyes, opened them a moment later to glance at her, then shut them again. Soon he was asleep.

She noticed that the bowl on the floor had broken neatly into two halves. Some of the oil had splashed onto the poetry book, staining its pages. It would be easy enough to clear it up now without disturbing him. But inertia set in and she didn't move for another hour.

SEVEN

It seemed to Tomas that he'd been lying submerged in the basin of the well for hours, having somehow floated up through cracks and crevasses in the strata of granite and quartz below. The water covering his body was warm and comforting, and the stone walls and vaulted roof held him in their mossy cradle. He could feel the massiveness of the earth, the distant void of sky beyond, but their weight and substance didn't affect him. He was at peace here, certain that nothing could reach him enclosed in this comforting darkness.

But then a tiny translucent thought appeared. It must have percolated up from the spring below, as he had done. It was eddying around his head, bumping against his face – his ears, his eyes, his nose, his mouth – trying to find a way in. It was such a curious thing: a cold, burning brightness that couldn't possibly be relevant to him. So he dismissed this thought and wouldn't let it in.

He kept his eyes closed, trying to ignore it, but somehow it found a way into his head. As soon as it had, he discovered that this insignificant little thought was shaped like the letter 'e'.

He opened his eyes.

Through the skylight he could see wisps of pink cloud drifting below an azure sky. They were called tailed cirrus clouds, he remembered – mares' tails. Gulls were crying high in the distance, and he could smell orange blossom. He knew where he was now, though not exactly how he'd come to be here.

Turning his head, which was wrapped in bandages, the room wobbled. Eventually he sat up, swung his legs round and, when he was sure he could manage it, stood up. He was wearing some sort of gown that barely covered his knees.

Jenna had her back to him, her hands clutching the drying rail of the Rayburn, watching the percolator brewing coffee. Her hair was tied back and she was wearing a thick woollen shirt, jeans and trainers.

'Hello.'

She spun round.

'God, you frightened me!' she gasped, then recomposed herself.

'How are you?'

He looked down at the floor, struggling for an answer. He didn't know how he was. The question seemed so invasive; he would have to make up a reply if he could. But he couldn't even manage that.

'May I use the bathroom?'

'Of course! Would you like some coffee?'

As he began nodding, a pain shot across his eyes and he flinched.

'Thank you,' he whispered, reaching for the bathroom door.

She filled two mugs and took them to the sitting room, then carried his folder to the bedroom.

What now? she wondered.

She felt tired and edgy. The thought of having to drive Tomas to hospital daunted her. She supposed Ester or Edward would do it if she asked, but... no, she would find the energy from somewhere.

Tomas appeared in the doorway, a curious sight in bandages and nightshirt.

'Who undressed me?'

She turned to look at him, bemused.

'You undressed yourself. Don't you remember?'

He looked at her with a dull expression she couldn't read.

'Coffee's in the sitting room.'

Then, seeing his bare feet, she asked, 'Do you want to get dressed first?' forgetting that his clothes weren't there.

'That's all right.' His speech was a bit slurred.

As he shuffled ahead of her through the conservatory she noticed that he was running the back of his hand along the wall, as if to steady himself.

They sat in the armchairs.

'I'm sorry about what happened,' he began.

'No, you mustn't... '

'I should never have come here.'

'Tomas... '

'Please let me say this!'

His stare was intense and disconcerting.

'I really wanted to meet you again. I thought I'd be okay; it was only a bump on the head. But I wasn't. I'm sorry to have made so much trouble. I'm going home now.'

'Hold on a minute!'

She felt a surge of annoyance that verged on anger.

'Yes, we were concerned, are concerned for you. But, you haven't been all that much trouble. Not yet anyway.

And you can't just wander off on your own. Arthur... Dr Sanders has arranged for you to have a scan at the hospital this morning. I'm taking you there.'

They looked intently at each other.

'How did it happen, anyway?'

'What?'

'Your injury.'

He hesitated. 'I hit my head on a cupboard.'

She avoided looking at him; he would see that she didn't believe him.

'On the corner of the kitchen cupboard. Early this morning. I mean yesterday morning.'

'The *back* of your head?'

'Yes!' He got up.

She quickly stood in front of him.

'Look, I'm sorry. It's none of my business. Sit down and drink your coffee.'

He remained where he was, glaring at her until she sat again. To her relief, he sat, too.

'I'm not going into hospital. I don't need to. I'm okay now.'

She sighed and sipped her coffee.

'They wanted to take you in last night.' She glanced at him. 'Maybe I should have let them.'

Holding the mug with both hands, he gulped down the coffee without stopping for breath, then banged the mug down on the table.

'I hate hospitals. What are they looking for, anyway?'

'They just want to make sure you're all right. They'll give your head a scan, which is the usual out-patient procedure when someone's had concussion. They're not going to admit you, Tomas, there's nothing to be frightened about.'

'I'm not frightened!'

She was feeling increasingly burdened by this boy, but having made herself responsible for him, she would have to see it through. What was making things more difficult was this change in his behaviour towards her. His moodiness and irritability were such a contrast to that over-anxious, well-mannered young man who had called on her yesterday afternoon.

There was a knock at the door, which made Tomas start from his chair.

'Come in,' Jenna called.

It was Ester, along with an excited Digory. She was carrying the bag of laundry and a first aid box.

'How's our patient this morning?' Beaming at Tomas, she crouched in front of the stove to face him.

'I'm okay.'

'Good. You slept all right, did you?'

'Yes.'

She continued, undeterred. 'Sorry about that big old bandage, Tomas. It's not very comfortable, is it?'

'It's okay.'

'I was thinking it would probably be a good idea to replace it with something a bit more modest, since you're going out in public. Save you getting funny looks. Can we do that?'

She opened the first aid box.

Jenna was grateful for the way her sister was able to handle Tomas. She managed to get his full co-operation, removing the bandage, making a cursory examination of the wound, then applying a fresh dressing and light bandage. And, after a lot of patient explanations and reassurances, he agreed to let Jenna take him to hospital.

The three of them had breakfast together, although

Tomas ate very little. While he was getting dressed, the sisters did the washing up.

'How are you, Jen?'

'Completely worn out. I've been up since five. Hardly slept at all before that.' She lowered her voice. 'The prospect of spending half the day with him in there doesn't exactly thrill me, either.'

'I'll do it.'

'What? No... '

'I'm not working until this evening. All I've got on is a visit to Dad this afternoon. I'll take him, Jen.'

She seriously considered the offer.

'Thanks, Ester, but I think I'd better see this through.'

'If you're sure.' She sounded disappointed.

'What about taking Digory along to Dad's? They'd enjoy a visit together.'

'All right, I'll do that.'

Jenna took Digory's lead from the hook inside the kitchen cupboard. As she handed it to her, Ester caught her eye.

'Can I have a quick word – outside?' she whispered.

Jenna called through the bedroom door.

'I'll be right back, Tomas.'

Ester began speaking as soon as she'd closed the door.

'I've spoken with Arthur. He'll be at the neuro unit if you can get there by midday.'

'Oh, that's marvellous. He must be exhausted, poor man.'

'He phoned very early. I wonder if he had any sleep at all.'

She felt an uneasy twinge.

'Why did he phone you?'

'He'd met Tomas and his family before.'

'When?'

'Mrs Lock was having treatment in his department until about eight months ago.'

'Was it...?'

'Cancer of the brainstem. Inoperable. She died last June.'

'How awful.'

'Aside from wanting you to be aware of that, if you didn't know already... '

'No, I hardly know anything about him!'

'The other thing he wanted to explain was why he'd agreed to let Tomas stay here last night rather than be taken home or into hospital. It wasn't just because the kid was making such a stink about it.'

'It did surprise me, frankly.'

'These brainstem tumours produce any number of symptoms,' she continued, 'but Arthur said the ones that affected his mother most were vomiting, dizziness, lack of co-ordination when walking, and difficulty in speaking.'

They had reached the barn. Jenna stopped and looked down at the ground, making sense of this.

'I see.'

'Arthur wasn't sure how he'd have coped, going into the same hospital with the same symptoms his mother had.'

She stroked Digory, who was getting impatient.

'And taking him home might have created other problems.'

'What do you mean?'

'The mother's death hit Tomas very hard, apparently, but father completely fell apart. There's an older daughter, who moved in with her boyfriend soon after mum died, leaving Tomas to cope on his own with a depressed, angry father – who's also a drinker.'

'God.'

'Arthur tried phoning him first thing this morning, thinking he might want to accompany his son into the scanning room, but he wasn't answering.'

She turned to look at Jenna.

'The kid's going to need a lot of support this morning. Do you think you'll be able to manage?'

'Yes, of course I will! I'll stay with him, then take him home.'

'Good. The other thing Arthur said is that he hasn't a clear picture of the cause of the injury. It could be that the father's abusive.'

'God, I hope not.'

'Anyway, take your mobile with you.'

Jenna prickled.

'Ester, please give me some credit!'

'It doesn't look like you'll be getting to Hendra today, does it? Do you want to give me the keys? I can drop them over.'

'Oh, God, I forgot!' she exclaimed. 'I still haven't found my diary. No, I'll go later this afternoon. It doesn't matter what time I get there.'

'Are you sure?'

'Yes, I'm sure!'

Jenna could see that they were now reaching the point where Ester might like to take over and manage her little sister as well.

'Would you tell Edward I won't be coming over for supper after all? I'm going to need an early night.'

'Yes, okay. Good luck, Jen.'

Ester followed Digory to the house.

When Jenna got back to The Fogou, Tomas was sitting by the stove. He had dressed and was wearing his coat and cap.

'I'm ready to go now,' he said without looking at her.

'I've just got to change first, if that's all right with you.'

As she said it, her phone rang. She was going to ignore it, but then thought it might be Tomas' father, so she went to the kitchen and answered it.

It was her editor, Pam, phoning from Moon Press in Falmouth.

'Hi, Jenna. How are you?'

'In a bit of a rush, at the moment. Otherwise, pretty shitty.'

'Oh. Sorry. I won't keep you. I've just found your half-yearly royalty cheque.'

'Found it?'

'In your file. I don't know why it didn't get sent off weeks ago. I'll have a word with Kim and make sure it's posted off today, first class.'

'Thanks, Pam. Look, while I've got you, has Conan mentioned anything about the *Sacred Cauldron* manuscript and poems I sent him? I haven't heard anything back from him.'

'Yes, I've just put them back in your file, as it happens. That's how I... '

'What did he say about them?'

She paused before answering. 'Look, there's nothing final about this, Jenna, but... I think Conan will be writing to you.'

'About the essay, or the poems?'

Pam was silent.

'He doesn't like any of it, does he?'

'I think he liked the poems. I certainly did! And he was impressed by the essay. But maybe not as a Moon Press publication.

'I see.'

'He said that if you tightened it up a bit and sent it to a journal – literary, or maybe something academic – they'd probably lap it up.'

'Take it elsewhere, he means.'

'He hasn't said so.'

'He will, though, won't he? I can feel it.'

'I'm sorry, Jenna, but things are pretty tight here at the moment, as you know.'

'Yeah, and I bet they'd be a lot tighter if Moon Press didn't have Jenna Mundey in its catalogue.'

'Well of course they would! You're not thinking of going somewhere else, are you?'

'I hadn't until a minute ago, but maybe I should. This really pisses me off, Pam!'

'I'm sure it does, but... '

'Moon's published other things besides poetry in the last few years.'

'Yes, but they're all directly relevant to Cornwall.'

'And Celtic literature isn't? Christ, is that what he thinks?'

'Look, I'm sorry. I shouldn't have said anything – but you did ask.'

'I know I did.'

'Wait and see what Conan has to say, all right.'

'Okay. I'm not going to do anything rash. I've got enough on my plate at the moment.'

EIGHT

Jenna stood waiting by the Mini, hoping she'd be warm enough in her roll-neck jumper, tweed trousers and linen jacket. The day was bright, but a chilly wind – carrying paint fumes from the open library doors – was brisk enough to be rippling the puddles on the track.

When Tomas caught up with her she noticed his trainers, wet and muddy. God, she should have walked beside him, taken his arm and steered him around the puddles.

She found herself being overly cautious, helping him into the car – standing by the open passenger door, holding a hand above his head in case he bumped it getting inside.

Once they'd set off, she realised that she was driving slower than usual, so she increased her speed.

As they approached Sancreed Church a young woman carrying a rucksack crossed the road, heading toward the footpath opposite, and Jenna braked unnecessarily. At the Penzance road she waited until she was sure there was no traffic approaching from either direction before pulling out.

She glanced at Tomas, who was staring ahead, no

discernible expression on his face. He hadn't spoken since the start of the journey.

'I wonder if that woman's going to the holy well,' she said, hoping to spark a bit of easy conversation.

'I was there this morning, or... yesterday, I think it was.' He continued to stare at the road.

'You think?'

'No, it was yesterday.'

'So was I.'

He glanced at her, then back at the road.

'I took Digory there for his early morning run. We often go that far.'

'For help?'

She was flustered by the bluntness of his question.

'I don't know, really. I love the setting – and the tradition of the holy well. I've always been drawn to the old places scattered around West Penwith. I think they can speak to you if you let them.'

'Yes.' He looked at her again. 'One or two of them speak to me sometimes.'

She tried to sound casual.

'Do they? What do they tell you?'

'They don't tell me anything. I don't mean it like that.' There was a hint of annoyance in his voice. 'They sort of... inspire me.'

'Yes, I see.'

After another silence he said, 'What did you ask for when you tied that purple cloutie onto the thorn tree?'

He sounded so matter-of-fact, she found herself doing a mental double-take. First she assumed she must have told him and forgotten, and then she realised that they hadn't spoken about the well until just now. She put her foot on the brake and slowed down.

A white delivery van, travelling too close behind, angrily flashed its headlights, so she accelerated again. She could feel her heart beating in her throat.

'How do you know about that, Tomas?'

'Your cloutie was the same as the woollen pull cords on your bedroom skylight.'

She didn't reply. The silence between them grew again.

'I'm sorry if you didn't want me to know.'

'No, it doesn't matter. You took me by surprise, that's all.'

'Sorry,' he repeated, sounding like a guilty child.

'Don't be sorry!'

She wished she wasn't so impatient with him.

They passed through the outskirts of Penzance, following the blue H signposts to the hospital.

'In a way... ' he said, 'I was at the well this morning.'

She had a sinking feeling and didn't reply at first. She turned into the car park behind the hospital and spotted a parking space.

'Just a minute, Tomas.'

She reversed into it and switched off the engine. When she turned to him again he was staring anxiously at the hospital buildings.

'What were you saying?'

'It doesn't matter.'

At reception in the radiology unit they were told they would have to wait, which they did for about fifteen minutes.

Jenna decided that she wouldn't try to make irrelevant conversation or pretend to read a magazine. So they sat silently in the waiting area. It was probably like every other one in this and every other hospital, smelling faintly of antiseptic and fear. It reminded her of the little room downstairs, just out of sight of the congested accident and emergency area, where she'd sat with her father twenty years ago, pretending to read a dog-eared issue of *The Lady*.

Father had sat like a stone, his eyes continually returning to the clock above the service area. The waiting had been interminable, with no one to answer their questions or explain what was happening. She'd held onto the magazine like an anchor when Father began sharing his anxieties with her.

Are they still working on her, do you think? Is she that bad? They're bound to keep her in, aren't they? Why don't they just tell us?

Where was Ester that day? At some academic interview somewhere. She would have been able to manage their father, with his growing suspicions and denials. All she could do was listen, struggling with her own fears.

Her father got up abruptly, announcing that he was going to the toilet and wouldn't be long. When he got back, she left it to the distressed young registrar to tell him that they'd done all they could, but they hadn't been able to start her mother's heart again...

When the radiography assistant appeared and called them both by name, Jenna attempted a smile and followed Tomas through to the treatment suite.

The MRI scan procedure was more of an ordeal than she'd imagined, and certainly a trying one for Tomas, despite the sensitivity of the staff. She hadn't anticipated that they would *both* have to complete and sign safety checklists, asking them about any medical conditions. The questions were mainly about metal implants, including one that asked whether she had a coil fitted.

They were led into separate cubicles. She left her

handbag and removed her watch, hair clasp, and silver ear studs. Tomas didn't have to undress, but took off his watch and belt.

The radiology room itself was intimidating. The huge, tubular machine dominated the space, and the sliding bed looked clinical and uninviting.

The technician told Tomas to lie on his back, as still as possible, and breathe normally. She explained that he would only be going into the machine as far as his head, and that once inside he would have to hold his breath at some points during the scan, moving as little as possible to prevent blurring. She fitted his earplugs and went out to the control panel.

When Jenna saw Arthur standing next to the radiologist she felt a huge surge of relief.

The loud vibrating noise inside the cylinder went on throughout the scan. When it was finally over, the assistant returned, helped Tomas down from the couch and removed the earplugs.

'That wasn't so bad, was it?'

Tomas didn't reply.

They met with Dr Sanders in his office in the neurology unit.

'I examined the images as we went along,' he told them, 'because if I hadn't they'd have been sent to your GP, Tomas, and you probably wouldn't have had the results for a fortnight.'

Tomas said nothing.

'I'll need to look at them again, but I honestly don't think I've missed anything. Nothing to worry about, anyway. There's no evidence of any lasting damage to the nerve tissue. You should be fine in a few days.'

'That *is* good news!' Jenna smiled at him, then at

Tomas, who hadn't been making eye contact with either of them.

'How are you feeling at the moment, Tomas?'

He shrugged.

'Headache?'

He nodded.

'Dizziness?'

He nodded again.

Arthur opened a filing cabinet drawer beside him and brought out a photocopied document of several pages, stapled together.

'This is a list of some of the impairments that a brain injury such as yours can temporarily cause.'

He handed it to Tomas, who reluctantly took it without even glancing at it.

'What I'd like you to do – not now, but over the next few days – is to read through the list and tick the boxes beside any of the ones that are troubling you. There may be a lot, or none at all, but what you can identify would be helpful to me when I see you again.'

Tomas dropped the questionnaire on the desk and folded his arms tightly against his chest.

Arthur and Jenna looked at each other, and then at him. He was scowling.

'Okay, so you never want to see me or this place again, is that it?'

Tomas said nothing.

'I can understand that. So, could we make a deal?'

Tomas remained silent.

'You do what I'm asking – make a record of how you're feeling – and in a couple of weeks you can either take it or send it to your GP, who knows you're here today. He'll pass it on to me for the records, and that will probably be the end of it. All right?'

Tomas looked at him, then glanced at Jenna, but didn't say anything.

'May I have a look?' Jenna asked them both.

Tomas pushed the paper across the desk to her, but Arthur took another copy from the filing cabinet.

'You can have one for yourself.'

She took a quick look at some of the questions, which were divided into categories such as Physical, Emotional and Intellectual.

'I probably shouldn't be telling you this... ' Arthur said. Tomas looked up at him with interest for the first time.

'Some of the staff here regularly use this checklist on themselves. Not because they've had concussion but, like most of us, they'd like to make some changes in themselves. It can be a useful tool.' Jenna looked down at the list and immediately spotted *anxiety*, *feeling isolated*, *dizziness*, and *temper outbursts*. She folded it in half and slipped it into her handbag.

'So, do we have an agreement, Tomas?'

'Okay,' he said reluctantly.

'Good. Now, get plenty of rest, and be sure there's someone keeping an eye on you, at least for the rest of today and tomorrow. That's really important. Don't strain yourself, and go easy on the alcohol.'

'I'll take him straight home and make sure he goes to bed,' Jenna assured the doctor.

Tomas gave a deep sigh as they left the hospital, and again when they were back in the car. Palpable relief that his ordeal was over.

Jenna didn't quite know what to say to him, so she said nothing.

As they were driving toward the hotel at Newlyn where Mr Lock worked, she wondered if they should stop and see if he was there. But when she glanced at Tomas, staring ahead at the road again, she didn't even suggest it.

At the far end of the village she considered taking the coastal road though Mousehole – up Raginnis Hill and past Castallack to Lamorna. She loved the view out to St Clement's Isle. But Tomas was probably preoccupied about getting home, so she kept to the B3315 and headed towards Paul.

Tomas' silence concerned her as much as his hostile behaviour had done this morning. Maybe she or Ester would be able to ask Arthur more about him. Or would that be a breach of professional ethics?

They had passed The Pipers and were approaching the Merry Maidens stone circle before she realised she'd driven past the turning to Lamorna Cove.

'Oh, how stupid!'

She pulled onto the narrow verge.

'I was miles away.'

'You can turn around there.'

Tomas was looking at the entrance to a field opposite.

She wrenched the wheel sharply to the right and crossed the lane. As they pulled up in front of a five-bar gate, he pointed to a large standing stone with a hole through it, now serving as a gatepost.

'I really like that stone.'

She looked at him, incredulous.

He continued staring at it, grinning to himself.

'Sometimes I used to find messages left in the hole. I put one in there myself once, when I was little, but I never got a reply.'

She switched off the engine.

'You amaze me, Tomas.'

He gave her a questioning look.

'What?'

'You've barely spoken to me since we left the hospital, so I assumed you were worrying about how things would be when you got home. You let me drive past your lane without so much as a word or a look in my direction, and now you're acting as if we're on some megalithic tour of West Penwith.'

He looked uncomfortable and she immediately wished she hadn't said anything.

'I'm sorry, I shouldn't have snapped at you. I... I'm tired.'

'That's all right.'

'No, it's not!'

She started the engine, reversed onto the road and drove back the way they'd come.

'When we get to your house I'd like to go in with you.'

'You don't have to do that.'

He was still sounding sullen.

'I know I don't, but I want to.'

She had to stop herself from placing a reassuring hand on his knee.

When he said nothing more she began worrying again. Despite the scan and Arthur's assurances, could there be some sort of malfunctioning as a result of the concussion?

Half way down the valley road, as they approached The Wink, she saw a man about to go into the pub and slowed down, almost to a stop.

Tomas looked at the man, who was now opening the door, then at Jenna.

'What?'

She shook her head and drove on.

It was Kitto. His studio was some way up the road

opposite. The last time she'd passed Well Lane she'd considered calling in on him, but had lost her nerve at the last minute.

Maybe she'd stop at The Wink after taking Tomas home. Running into him would just be a coincidence. It could have happened at any time over the past five months.

'You can park there,' Tomas told her.

They'd reached the bottom of the hill and he was pointing to an unmade lay-by between the row of cottages and the sea wall car park.

As soon as she turned off the ignition, he got out and slammed the door. A chill hung in the air. She looked over the grey little harbour to the huge quay. The tide was out, but its wet shadow was traceable on the bright green of boulders and smaller stones edging the shoreline. She felt that huge potent presence of the sea beyond the port, which always affected her. She sighed.

The Locks' cottage, grey and weathered like the others in the row, seemed to radiate less life. What had Tomas said about living here? It can feel sort of empty.

She caught up with him as he was unlocking the front door. It opened onto a narrow hallway, doorways left and right, and a steep flight of uncarpeted stairs. She followed him through the living room, dominated by a large grey television and an overstuffed grey sofa, into the kitchen.

'Wait here a minute.'

He turned and went upstairs.

She looked around the dim little room. A square table, covered with a faded blue PVC cloth, and four chairs were the only furniture. She noticed a framed sampler, hanging on the wall next to the back door:

As Thy Days, So Shall Thy Strength Be.

On the counter a pair of knitted gloves, one rolled inside the other, sat on top of a fat, black, leather-bound notebook.

She noticed there was only one hanging cupboard and scrutinised its height and position between the stove and refrigerator. She didn't see how it could have been the source of Tomas' injury.

On the table was a piece of paper, torn into squares and stacked into a pile. She picked up the top one and read: *Mundey's. Maybe somewhere...* Hearing his footsteps, she quickly put it back.

Tomas' face was impassive. He surprised her by dragging out a chair and flopping down onto it. He sat looking at his folded hands resting on the table. She sat as well.

'He isn't here.'

'Wouldn't he be at work?' she asked. 'Shouldn't we phone him?'

He shook his head.

'Or, we could drive there... '

'No.'

When he saw the torn-up note he grabbed the pieces and dropped them into the rubbish bin, watching them slide down between the stained tea towel and the rum bottle.

He angrily snatched up his notebook, stared at it for a moment, then slid it into his coat pocket.

'You can go now. I'll be okay.'

He leaned back against the counter.

'No, I can't go yet, Tomas.'

Standing to face him, the scene reminded her of their altercation this morning, when he had also seemed determined to go off on his own.

'Doctor Sanders said you shouldn't be left alone today, didn't he?'

He stood there looking helpless, as though waiting for her to tell him what to do.

She couldn't think of a way through this; she wished she could walk out of here and drive half way up the hill to The Wink. She considered several options, then dismissed each one in turn. She certainly wouldn't contact Tomas' father against his will. Nor would she ask him if he had family or friends nearby – or even neighbours he could spend the day with. It would sound as though she were trying to off-load him, which of course she was, in a way.

The silence between them lengthened. She remembered Ester asking her if she'd be able to manage. Somehow she was going to have to see this through.

'Tomas, would you be willing to come back and stay with me for another day?'

'What!'

He reacted as though she had sexually propositioned him, and looked away. She didn't repeat the question, which hung in the air for what seemed a long time. He shook his head again.

'Before you say no,' she said, thinking on her feet, 'let me tell you about the rest of my day.'

She sat again and he edged toward the table. Now she might have caught his attention.

'I've got to go to Morvah briefly, so I thought I might stop for some lunch at St Buryan. Then back to The Fogou later this afternoon. If you were staying over I'd want to sort out the guest room, make it a bit more comfortable. Do you cook at all?'

He nodded and sat opposite her.

'I'll probably make a vegetable stew or something for supper. Later I might spend an hour preparing for a reading I'll be doing in Cardiff in the spring. I'd appreciate your thoughts, since you were at the last one. Or you could spend some time on your own. Read or listen to some music. Maybe write up your notes from our interview.'

He nodded again.

'I usually take Digory out for a run on the moor after supper. Then bed down the stove for the night... '

There was silence again. She found herself listening to the ticking of the clock on the wall as she watched him.

'I don't know.'

'What would you be doing otherwise, Tomas?'

'Nothing much.' He looked miserable.

'I'd like you to come with me.'

He said nothing.

'Why don't you put a few things in a bag and leave a note for your father. Or you could phone him.'

She immediately wished she hadn't mentioned his father. 'In fact, don't even bother with that. He has my mobile number if he wants to be in touch.'

He stood up, but didn't move.

'Okay.'

When he turned, heading for the stairs, she felt her tension easing. But then he saw the red flashing light on the answering machine. He stopped and pushed the button.

'*Hello, this is Jenna Mundey speaking.*'

Jenna cringed.

Tomas looked at her, amazed, then back at the machine.

'*I hope I've reached the home of Tomas Lock – who attends Penzance College? I'm sorry to be phoning at such short notice Tomas, but I wonder if it would be possible for us to rearrange this afternoon's interview? Maybe for next Sunday? I'll give you my mobile number.*' Digory started barking.

'*Hold on... it's 07814 103651. I'm very sorry, Tomas. Things are a bit chaotic here at the moment – as you can hear! But I do look forward to meeting you. Shall we say in a week's time? Goodbye for now.*'

He was still staring at the machine when a second message began.

'*Hey, Tomas, where the hell are you?*' Lorca paused. '*Are you there?*' Another pause. '*You're not still pissed off with me about this morning, are you? I really couldn't help it mate. Anyway, how did it go with Mizz Mundey? I want all the details. Was she just as...*'

He switched off the machine.

Jenna stood up. 'Tomas, I should have told you... '

'Forget it.' He turned and went to the stairs.

'No, please! I lost my diary, and I didn't... '

'It doesn't matter! *Forget it!*' he shouted.

Tomas' bedroom was as he'd left it yesterday, as far as he could remember. He went to the chest of drawers. The stack of letters that his father had gone through on Saturday night, the few from Tamsyn and the rest from Lorca, were back in the top drawer.

He lifted out the tin box lying under the handkerchiefs at the back of the bottom drawer and opened it. He would take all the money with him, since his father was drinking again. He folded the notes together and shoved them into his back pocket.

The rucksack he dragged out from under his bed was dusty. He'd only ever used it for when he was staying with his grandparents, and that hadn't been this year – or last year. He packed a change of clothes, and the bright paisley handkerchief his sister had given him for Christmas. Then he went to the window. Looking out at the high granite wall, he couldn't see any of the faces that had been there yesterday, and wondered if this was a good omen. He hoped so, because everything had been a disaster since then. He pressed his forehead against the glass and bumped his head, experimentally, against the pane. Then again. And again. Each time harder than the last.

Standing there, he went over everything he could remember about yesterday, last night and this morning. He had never so completely lost control or acted so stupidly, except maybe at the funeral. Had he actually kicked out at the doctor last night? He thought he had.

Even if all this wasn't all his fault, that wasn't the point. Why had he gone to The Fogou in the first place? He should have known he wouldn't make it through the day. Lorca's phone call and the dead motorcycle should have stopped him. But he'd selfishly forced himself to go, and he'd crashed into her life like a road accident. Christ!

She should have told him that it wasn't a good time when he got there. He would have come home, gone back to bed, and none of it would have happened. He hated being in situations where he felt vulnerable, and he wasn't used to it – except with his father, of course. Or being dependent on other people – except with Lorca sometimes.

He'd acted so stupidly. And then his stroppiness with her this morning! Why was he being like this? He thought things would be easier between them after the hospital, but hearing her telephone message, saying that she didn't want him to come in the first place, made it worse. Now she'd be stuck with him for another bloody day, but not because she wanted to – obviously. She probably thought he was some kind of freak – some deranged, dim-witted teenager – which was the last thing he wanted to be in her eyes.

If he refused to go with her she couldn't force him. She'd probably be relieved! But... *what would you be doing otherwise?* He hadn't a clue. If he could just cool down now, stop being such a burden to her, maybe he would have the chance to put things right between them.

He took the letters from the chest of drawers, stuffed them into his rucksack and zipped it shut.

Jenna was waiting in the kitchen. He told her he was ready and they very nearly smiled at each another.

'I'll need to make a phone call later this afternoon, if that's all right,' he said.

'Of course. No problem.'

Passing the answering machine on their way out, he pressed the delete button.

NINE

During the short drive to St Buryan, Tomas certainly felt more clear-headed; the headache was virtually gone. The midday sky was a bright, bird's egg blue, and the fields looked incredibly fresh and green. He would buy Jenna lunch.

They parked next to the old Celtic cross in front of the church. He looked up at the tall tower – holding the heaviest peal of six bells in the world! He loved listening for them at his bedroom window every Sunday morning.

He'd been inside St Buriana's church more than any other in West Penwith, but never on a Sunday. What drew him there was the carved wooden rood screen, even more beautiful than the one at Sancreed. He would carefully examine every detail of the intricate carvings that covered it: the motifs of vine and oak leaves, the grinning heads, the strange little battles taking place between birds and animals. The screen, once painted shades of red and blue, was still gilded on parts of the cornice, and the faded colours were soft and warm now. He'd sit gazing at it all – as if it was the most subtle and glorious sunset imaginable. And it would all still be there waiting for him the next time he returned.

'Did you want to go inside?' Jenna asked, tucking her cold hands deeper into her jacket pockets.

He shook his head and pulled down his cap to cover the bandage.

They crossed the road to the St Buryan Inn.

Fish and chips were on the menu, but when Jenna ordered a Stilton ploughman's he wondered if she was a vegetarian and decided to have the same. Then she refused to let him pay for their food and drinks, telling him that it was her treat. He stubbornly insisted that he didn't want her to, so in the end they each awkwardly paid for their own.

The bar was half-empty this Monday lunchtime. They sat at the far corner table, with glasses of sparkling apple juice, waiting for their food to arrive.

'Tomas, what did you mean earlier when you said you were at Sancreed Well this morning?'

He'd known that she would come back to this sooner or later. He sighed, tracing lines of bubbles through the moisture on his glass, thinking he'd better try to explain.

'I don't know how to describe it. You'll think I'm mad.'

He waited for some sign of encouragement from her, but there wasn't any. He supposed he'd better carry on anyway.

'I guess I must have been delirious. I had this amazing... it wasn't a dream, exactly. A kind of experience.'

'What sort of experience?'

Their food arrived, so he waited until after he'd had his first mouthful.

'I was lying underwater inside the well. After a while something came swimming up from the bottom – like a tadpole, shiny and transparent. I know it sounds stupid, but it turned out to be a thought.'

She held her knife poised midair.

'What do you mean?'

'It was a thought. You know – an idea. It was trying to get inside my head, and when it did it made me understand something I couldn't have realised on my own.'

She looked uneasy. 'What was that?'

He took another bite of bread and cheese, wondering how to go on.

'*Bimarian Ground...* '

Their eyes locked.

'Go on,' she said.

'You told me that you wrote it in lipograms because you were having trouble with your "e"s.'

'That's right, I did.'

'Then you said you were only joking, but my thought told me... ' He hesitated.

'Go on.'

He reached for his glass and held onto it.

'I suddenly knew what you meant. That you'd been having trouble – some kind of trouble – with Edward and Ester. And Ebril?'

Jenna looked stunned and blinked her eyes.

'God, how amazing. I've been found out.'

So it's true!

He didn't know what else to say. He'd uncovered a secret, and now it couldn't be hidden again.

'I'm sorry. I shouldn't have told you.'

'Don't be silly.' She reached over and rested a hand on his.

'It's just so extraordinary. And the way you describe it happening. You could write a poem about it.'

'I don't think so.'

He could never write about the well – not the one in his

dream, and not the actual holy well itself. Either way it would be a betrayal.

'What are you thinking?'

He blushed, looking at his empty glass.

'When we were talking in the car – about Sancreed Well – I started thinking about why I go there. Whether it's for healing or inspiration.'

'And which is it?'

'I don't think I know the difference any more.'

He pushed his empty plate aside.

'I can't imagine other people using it the way I do. But, "using" isn't the right word. I'm sure people do use places like that: abuse them – like drugs or alcohol. Religion, even. Giving themselves a fix when something's missing in their lives. I mean... '

He was speaking too fast, saying too much and too little at the same time.

'God, I don't know what I mean. Forget it.'

He placed his empty glass on the plate and folded his hands in his lap. 'I'm talking rubbish.'

'No, don't give up.'

If he didn't try to explain she might think he was playing some kind of mind game with her, which he certainly wasn't.

'Okay. When I go to the well, I always... I can't write at home. I can't be creative about anything there. Living with my father is like... soul-destroying! It's not all his fault, but when... Shit.'

'When...?'

'That's not what I was going to say, either.'

'Take your time.'

He closed his eyes, then opened them and glanced at her. She was waiting.

Be honest!

'Whenever I decide to go to the well, something starts off in my head and I get keyed up, anticipating being there. I used to think it could give some healing to my mother, and to me, which was stupid.'

'No, Tomas.'

He took a deep breath, looked to see if she was uncomfortable and decided that she wasn't.

'Now when I go there, I hope it will trigger me into writing a poem. And it usually does. Only the start of a verse, or maybe the last couplet of a sonnet – something I have to take away to finish by myself. It happens almost every time now. It just happens, and I don't need to tie a cloutie onto the tree, or make a prayer or anything, but I do that, too. All I need is someplace quiet afterwards to finish the poem. And when I do, I feel like I've been blessed by the well or something.'

'You are blessed, Tomas.' Jenna was smiling, almost affectionately. 'You should finish your poem. You could work on it tonight, while I'm... '

'What poem?'

She felt her face flush and looked across the room. A group of young people had come bursting into the bar, talking loudly and laughing together. She looked back at Tomas.

'Now I'm afraid it's my turn to apologise. I read the lines you wrote on the paper in your folder. I shouldn't have. I'm sorry.'

'That's all right.'

He felt exposed and was riding a swell of anger.

'I'm getting used to it. My father helps himself to whatever's mine whenever he wants to, so feel free!'

She looked aghast.

'Oh, Tomas, no! Please! I don't know how I could have done such a thing.'

Now he was watching the group of young people at the bar, something pounding in his head.

One of the girls from his sociology class raised her eyebrows, probably shocked to see him with this intense older woman. She grinned and waved, flashing glossy black fingernails at him, but he ignored her. She was with one of the tougher college boys – who'd once bullied him in front of a teacher.

'It's okay,' he said, louder than he intended. 'It doesn't matter. Are you ready to go?'

He watched her putting on her jacket, struggling with one of the sleeves. He unfolded it for her and held the collar while she slipped into it. She looked more fragile doing up the buttons, not so buoyant or youthful.

Christ, he'd done it again!

TEN

Neither of them spoke until after they had passed through Pendeen.

'Why are we going to Morvah?' he asked.

'I have to return some keys. It won't take long.'

Just after Bojewyan she turned the car left onto a rough track. A minute later they pulled up in front of a stone farmhouse. The slate sign on the gatepost read: *Hendra*.

'Whose farm is this?'

'It was ours. My family's smallholding.'

She turned off the engine and took an envelope from the shelf under the console.

'I found some of the original keys when I was moving into The Fogou and want the new owners to have them.'

He continued gazing at the farmhouse, thinking that it was very beautiful – traditional and compact, with a barn attached at one end and another farm building at the other.

'I'll be two minutes. Turn on the radio if you like – or there are some CDs in the tray.'

She hurried through the front gate. He watched her tear open the envelope and take out a set of large old-fashioned keys. A smartly dressed young woman opened the door before she knocked and led her inside. The woman didn't look like a farmer.

The large blocks of granite that made up all the buildings needed repointing, giving the impression that they were held together more by gravity than mortar. The place was very old, and the new owners very new. He wondered whether they'd bought it as a holiday home – the fate of so many properties in Cornwall.

When he was younger, and had a whole day free to himself, Tomas would set off on his bicycle, exploring West Penwith from Lamorna to Land's End and every-where between the two coasts. He'd stop to gaze at a traditional farmstead or an isolated outbuilding that caught his eye just as he would at standing stones, cairns and ancient settlements. Sometimes he'd write poems about them.

He wondered how it might feel to ride through the lanes on a motorbike. But he didn't have a motorbike, and wasn't going to have one.

After sitting impatiently for several minutes he decided that he'd waited long enough and got out of the car. He went in through the gate, crossed a patch of lawn and a small orchard, then skirted round a neglected flower and vegetable garden at the side of the house.

A steep flight of stone steps led up to a solid wooden door on the first floor of what might once have been the dairy or grain store. He climbed to the top and bent down to peer through the large keyhole, but only saw the darkness inside.

He was sitting on the top step, listening to the faint sound of the sea in the near distance, when Jenna appeared from around the corner.

'What are you doing?'

She sounded like Edward did when they'd met on the drive.

'I asked you to wait in the car.'

She looked annoyed or worried, he couldn't tell which.

'I'll only be another minute.'

When she went back inside he returned to the car and stood impatiently beside it, waiting. Two minutes later she came out.

'I didn't know where you'd gone.'

Obviously, she doesn't trust me, he thought.

They were looking warily at one another.

He didn't say anything and she didn't move toward the driver's door.

'Do you want to walk for a bit, or have you done too much already today? Should we go back?'

He shook his head. 'I could hear the sea from up there.'

She turned and pointed to an upstairs window.

'That was my room, on the left. I always kept the window ajar, even in winter, just for that sound.'

She smiled warmly and he felt reassured.

'Come on. We won't go far.'

There were no buildings beyond Hendra, and the track soon became a bridleway. They followed a stream until it ran onto the shore at Portheras Cove, then took the coastal path that skirted the little beach. The strand was deserted, except for a seagull poking at an abandoned plastic sandwich container.

She went on ahead, up to Kenidjacks cliff top, looking back once to make sure he was following.

A bracing breeze blew at them as they stood together at the top, watching great Atlantic rollers pounding onto the shore.

They continued westward until she stopped at a

footpath. From here they could see Pendeen Watch and, eastward, the long ragged run of high cliffs beyond Blinker's Bed, plunging straight down into the sea.

'Ester and I spent so much of our childhoods here – all along this path and down at the cove. We loved watching the seals and playing games in that little valley.'

She looked out at The Wra, a chain of half-submerged rocks beyond the harbour, as if searching for something there.

'We called those rocks The Serpent. Can you see how they make the shape of a sea monster swimming in toward the shore?'

Tomas said that he could.

'When I wanted to be on my own, I'd go up there.'

She gestured toward the path that led to Pendeen House.

'Our neighbours would let me explore the fogou on their farm. Pendeen Vau was my secret hiding place.'

'There's a fogou at the top of Lamorna Vale – at Boleigh.'

'Yes, I know that one, too, but Pendeen Vau is much longer. I used to crawl into it with a torch or a candle. Where the tunnel turns there's quartz embedded in the wall that would sparkle as I went past. I'd go in another thirty feet, except when it was too muddy – to where the central passage meets the side chambers. I'd sit there imagining I could feel the weight of those huge flat stones that make it a cave, holding me safe.'

'That sounds like my dream in the well.'

'Does it?'

They had gone far enough.

During the drive back to Chyangwyns, Tomas was thinking about Hendra, the old farmstead.

'Are your parents dead?'

'My father's alive. Eighty-one and mentally fit, but he

had a couple of worrying falls. A year ago last September he began complaining that it was too much for Ester and me to be looking after him night and day and he decided we should sell up. "Disperse," he called it. We were very lucky to find sheltered accommodation for him around here.'

'You were living at Hendra?'

'Ester lived with my father and I joined them for a while, yes.'

She glanced at him and was silent for a moment, considering how much more she should tell him – or whether she'd said too much already. Maybe taking him to Hendra wasn't such a good idea. It always brought her back in touch with difficult times as well as the idyllic ones.

'Edward suffers from clinical depression. Which hasn't been easy to live with – for either of us.'

She glanced at him again.

'I guess you know about that, don't you? What did you call the atmosphere at home? Soul-destroying?'

Tomas didn't reply.

'So I retreated back to Hendra. I'd had an accident, then some medical complications. Ester's very good with people in crisis. In fact she seems to thrive on the dis-ease around her.'

Tomas flinched and Jenna noticed.

'Sorry, that was crass. An obtuse thing to say.'

'It's okay.'

'What I meant is that she's very good when someone's "uneasy" – needing support.'

'I understand.'

'She dropped out of pre-med, did nursing, then trained as a therapist. Now she's co-ordinator at The Minerva.'

'Minerva?'

'A women's counselling centre in Penzance.'

He wanted to ask why only women, but didn't.

'Is that when she came to Chyangwyns? When you "dispersed"?'

'No, she moved in with her friend Bethan, who wanted someone to share her large house in Lamorna. It wasn't a good idea for either of them. Bethan works as a counsellor at Minerva, and they ended up talking shop too much of the time.

'I invited her to come to stay with us for a while, and she agreed. Then – I don't really know how it happened – there she was living with us. It's worked because there've been advantages for all three of us. She's much better with Edward than I am. Incredibly buoyant and determined when someone needs her loving support.'

She parked the Mini in the carriage house and they walked together, side by side, to The Fogou.

'Aha!'

On top of the coal bunker was her first weekly organic veg delivery. Tomas picked up the wooden crate while she unlocked the door.

'Just put it on the kitchen counter.' Then: 'Oh, but you shouldn't be doing that, Tomas! I'd forgotten.'

'So had I.'

He slid the box onto the counter. 'I feel okay now.'

She took his coat, and went to hang it over the bedroom chair. He followed, set his rucksack by the bed and squeezed past her to get the notebook from his coat pocket. Then he worried she might think he didn't trust her after she'd confessed to reading his poem, so he trailed after her, back to the kitchen.

'I needed a telephone number,' he lied, holding up the

notebook. 'Would you mind if I use your phone now?'

'Of course not. It's in my handbag.'

While she was getting it, he read the note lying on top of the pile of mail on the counter:

Hope the little blighter's safely tucked up. You can relax now! Give me a shout when you come over for Digory and tell me how it all went.
Edward's fine today!
E.

'Use the sitting room.'

Startled, he dropped the note. She handed him the phone and began filling the kettle.

'Would you like a cup of tea?'

'No, thank you.'

There was only a faint glow in the firebox, so he piled a few bits of kindling and two logs on top of the embers. When it caught he lifted the phone and punched in the numbers.

As Jenna came through the conservatory he cancelled the call and looked up at her.

'I'm going over to the house to fetch Digory. Make yourself comfortable, I'll be back soon.'

Hearing the kitchen door close, he redialled. It only rang twice.

'*Casa Lorca.*'

'Hey, amigo, it's me.'

'Where the hell have you been, Tomas?'

'How long have you got?'

ELEVEN

The paint was dry. Edward and Ester were putting books back onto the library shelves when Jenna came in. There was some minor dispute going on about how far they should take the reorganisation. Jenna had taken all her books to The Fogou, and now they needed to accommodate Ester's considerable collection, as well as those that had belonged to their parents, still in boxes somewhere upstairs.

It was obvious that Edward was in better spirits than yesterday. He beamed at her when she came in and kissed her lightly on the cheek.

'How's the boy?' he asked, sliding a hand down her back and settling it just below her waist.

'Yes, how'd it go, Jen?'

'He's recovering. There's been no lasting damage to the nerves apparently, so nothing to worry about long-term.'

'Excellent,' Ester said.

'He's staying with me for another night, though.'

Ester arched her brows. 'Oh? Why's that?'

Thinking she heard a critical judgement in the question, Jenna found herself searching for some covert motive or naïve misjudgement her sister might have spotted. When she couldn't find any, the insinuation annoyed her.

'I don't know what his father's up to, for a start. He wasn't at the cottage, and he hasn't contacted me. I couldn't just leave him there on his own.'

'No, of course not,' Edward said, protectively.

'Have you actually tried phoning the father? Or left a message for him at work? Surely, he should be... '

'There's more than a bump on the head troubling him, Ester.'

'You shouldn't underestimate delayed post-concussion symptoms,' she said with authority.

Jenna was becoming agitated.

'He says he doesn't feel sick or dizzy now, and the headache's gone. He had a decent lunch, and he's much more responsive than he was this morning. Still a bit prickly, though.'

Ester lifted a fat book from a tea chest, opened it to the index, then flipped through to the page she was looking for.

'Quote: Post-concussive symptoms may persist for some weeks. During this time the patient may experience any number of changes reflective of insult to the brain, including low frustration tolerance, poor concentration, muddled thinking, depression, uncontrolled emotions, altered levels of consciousness, fatigue, amnesia, irritability, anxiety, memory problems, disorientation... '

'Okay, stop! I'm aware of all that!' She glared at her. 'But, someone else is going to have to look after him tomorrow, whatever shape he's in. *My* life needs a bit of looking after, too!'

Neither Ester nor Edward responded. The room became very quiet until Digory put his head around the half-open door and sauntered in.

As soon as Jenna knelt and caressed Digory's neck, her anger softened.

'Hello, Digs.'

'He's had a good run today,' Ester told her.

'How's Dad?'

'Fine. Aunt Roz was just leaving when I arrived. They'd been playing cards and having a good old chin-wag. They both send their love.'

'Thanks. I'll try to get over later in the week.'

'What about supper tonight, Jen?' Edward asked.

'Didn't Ester tell you?' She glanced at her sister.

'Of course I did!'

'I was only thinking, wouldn't it be easier if you and the kid came over here for a meal?' he continued. 'Nothing fancy, and just the three of us. It would save you the bother of having to rustle up something yourself.'

'Three of us?'

'I've got a supervision group tonight,' Ester said, looking at the books on a half-filled shelf.

'Of course. No, I think we'd better see the day through on our own, Edward. I've already told him I'll be making a meal, and I don't want to confuse him or make him feel more... whatever it is.'

Ester was lifting the last few books from a tea chest. 'But you don't have to mollycoddle him either.'

'I *know* that, Ester! Just back off, please!'

She rose, clutching the books. 'I beg your pardon?'

'It's you who's just been lecturing to me about symptoms, for God's sake!'

Cutting into this confrontation, Edward asked, 'Tomorrow night then?'

'What?' When Jenna realised what he was asking she replied, 'Yes, okay – supper tomorrow. The *three* of us, is it?'

'If that's a problem, I could always... ' Ester began.

'Come on, Digory.'

Heading back to The Fogou, Jenna was fuming with frustration and anger. If only Ester would stop being so smug! But what chance was there of that happening? She should go straight back and tell them to forget about supper tomorrow.

She should have been writing today, working on *The Sacred Cauldron*, and considering whether or not to look for another publisher, much as she hated the idea.

She heard a squeal.

Directly ahead of her, on the edge of the moor, a large bird was flying low over the heather, searching for prey. Its pale plumage and black-tipped wings made it unmistakable: the hen harrier. She'd seen it yesterday morning on her way over to check on the hens – ironically – and now here it was again.

She wanted to follow it. Would she be missed if she went for a walk over Bartinney Downs for just half an hour? She'd take Digory, maybe go as far as Caer Brân – they often saw the hen harrier hunting there. Or a bit further? To the long fogou and holy wells at the Carn Euny settlement...

But it would be dark before she got back. She could imagine Tomas trying to light one of the oil lamps, just for the novelty of it, and damaging the mantle. They're so delicate, and expensive. Anyway, he shouldn't really be on his own.

Turning into the stable yard, she noticed how effectively the *Amaranthus* plants in the conservatory screened the interior at this time of day.

It felt odd, thinking that someone was there in The Fogou without her. For months she'd fought for a place of her own. It had been hard-won and – who knows? – it might not last. You can't know how a thing will end until it's ended – and sometimes not even then, her mother used to say. The same was true of beginnings, which are often only seen with hindsight.

A virtual stranger arrives one day and is foisted upon your life by unforeseen circumstances. The next day he's still there, making use of your home – probably sitting by your stove right now, talking to someone else you don't really know on *your* mobile phone.

Digory gave a loud, scolding bark when he saw a shadowy figure pass though the conservatory, heading for the kitchen.

'That's *right*! Good boy!' she told him, giving his back a mighty pat.

Tomas had made a pot of tea after all, and was helping himself to the spicy biscuits. He looked more relaxed than he had earlier. Apparently his brief respite from her had done him more good than hers from him.

Ester's note was still on the counter. She tore it into pieces and threw it into the Rayburn. When Tomas asked, 'Is Edward okay today?' she realised that he had read it.

'Yes, he's fine.'

Digory spotted the biscuits and was making a fuss over Tomas.

'Can he have a bit?' He broke off a corner.

She shook her head. 'No sugar.'

He went to the sink and rinsed out his teacup. He had a very serious, critical expression on his face, which she couldn't read, and it bothered her.

'Tomas?'

He turned to look at her.

'What is it? What are you thinking?'

'Aren't you jealous?' he blurted out.

She didn't understand.

'Jealous?'

'Your *sister* and your *husband*...'

Now she understood. She eventually shrugged, not wanting to get into this discussion.

'Occasionally, I suppose, but certainly not at the moment,' she said glibly.

'Sorry. It's just that... '

'Anyway, if sex is what you mean, the answer's no. Ester's a lesbian.'

He blushed and looked away. 'Oh, I see.'

It was obvious that his embarrassment was not about Ester's sexuality. It was about her indiscretion in telling him.

'God, I shouldn't have said that. It was totally inappropriate.'

'That's all right.'

'No, it's not, but it's too late now. I'm... I've not really settled here yet and it's making me rattled. I keep reminding myself that it's early days, to give it time.'

'Give what time?'

'Everything – all of it – but the move in particular. I've only been here a week, Tomas.'

'A week!'

'You're my first visitor.'

He shook his head, incredulous. 'I should never have... '

'Stop! Don't say it.'

As she poured herself a cup of stewed tea she suddenly remembered lines from a Levertov poem and was unable to shake them off:

Just when you seem to yourself
nothing but a flimsy web
of questions, you are given
the questions of others to hold
in the emptiness of your hands...
as if they were answers
to all you ask.

'Anyway, Tomas, did you have any luck?'

'What?'

'Your phone call?'

'Oh. Yes, I made two. I'll pay you for them.'

'Don't be silly. You spoke with your father?'

She could see from his expression that he hadn't. He shook his head.

'I phoned my friend Lorca. He's coming down from Exeter tonight and staying with his family at Longrock for a few days. And my sister's coming home for a while. We're all going out for a Mexican meal tomorrow night.'

'Tomas, I forgot! It's your birthday tomorrow, isn't it?'

'Yes.' He gave her an embarrassed grin.

It struck her again that he looked, and at times certainly acted, younger than his nineteen years. There was that blend of shyness and petulance about him; and a deep seriousness tinged with sadness that seemed to weigh on his young shoulders.

'Would it be all right if I rest for a while?'

'I was going to suggest it.' She was remembering 'fatigue' from Ester's list of symptoms. 'Go back to my bed for now.'

'I'm sorry to be putting you to so much trouble.'

Jenna put her hands on her hips and tilted her head.

'You know, we seem to be spending a lot of time

apologising and saying we're sorry to each other. Have you noticed, Tomas?'

'Yes.'

'Maybe we should stop now.'

'Yes. Okay.'

TWELVE

Once Tomas was out of the way, Jenna began reclaiming possession of herself and her Fogou – at least as much as the obligations of hospitality permitted.

She stripped the bedding from the futon in the stable room, where she'd hardly slept last night. Having finally dozed off, not much before dawn, she'd woken twice from disturbing dreams.

She laid fresh linen over the rug rail to air, then brought in an oil lamp, set it on one of the stools from the music room and placed a few poetry books on the other stool.

The room looked comfortable, she decided, putting a jug of water and a glass on the pine box. But the walls were rather stark, and Ebril's poem seemed too dominant. She lifted down Kitto's painting of Sancreed Beacon and carried it back to the guest room, as she would now call it, and propped it against the back wall.

Her phone lay on the kitchen counter. She opened it to the directory, and there it was: K for Kitto, and his mobile number. She dialled it and listened. When his soft voice said hello she drew in a breath and ended the call, relieved that it had only been his recorded message.

What would she have said to him? What *would* she say

if he returned her call? Maybe that she'd heard from Ester that his landlady, Bethan, was away this week – somewhere in Pembrokeshire. And when she'd driven past Well Lane this morning she'd wanted to drop in on him. Make up some excuse why she couldn't. She'd never lied to him before – although she'd lied several times because of him, and had hated doing it. Anyway, he might have seen her this morning when she'd drawn up outside The Wink. He probably would have recognised her Mini.

How could she have considered going back to the pub, hoping he'd still be there, after leaving Tomas? It must have been the dullness of her tired mind. At least she hoped that's all it was.

She took a sip of her cold, acrid tea and poured the rest of it down the drain. She was thinking about the converted 'pilchard palace' near Sennen where she and Kitto had stayed, eighteen months ago, while his friends Nick and Sara were on holiday. It was an extraordinary place, right on the shore, only accessible on foot or by boat.

Over the courtyard, where pilchards had once been cured and pressed, Nick had created a glassed-in studio, with slate steps leading up to the bright galleried bedroom and bath. Outside there were sunken gardens, originally salt cellars, with fantastic views of the sea. In the sheltered cove, with a stony little beach, they'd swum naked.

Ester and Father presumed she'd gone back to Chyangwyns to test the water with Edward, while he supposed that she was still at Hendra. She was barely eight miles from any of them. This secret assignation had made her feel culpable and tense, except when they were making love, and they made love often.

Kitto had recently returned from Spain, where he'd been living for a few months, in a mountain village somewhere south of Granada. He was staying with his parents in Newlyn, getting a crop of recent paintings together for the gallery and considering where to go next. He could please himself, and his free spirit, so much a part of him, always gave her surreptitious pleasure.

It was her inability simply to live in the moment without worrying about the consequences, as he seemed to do so naturally, that had ended their affair. She'd been unwilling to let go of the security of a home base, however fragile and unsatisfactory, in exchange for passion and freedom.

Now she found herself wondering, *why ever not?* Her marriage had become one in which there was loyalty without passion, a measured amount of independence without freedom, and a kind of equilibrium that enabled her at times to be creative.

She riddled the Rayburn, emptied the ash and clinkers into one of the two tin ash boxes outside the door, and carried it around to the back. The gritty garden path was spongy underfoot. She dumped the tin's contents into the largest puddle and tamped them down with the base of the box.

The sun was setting – dull, grey and murky – at the edge of the moor. She snapped off two drooping blades of chives and chewed on them.

On their last but one day together, she and Kitto had sat on the shore, watching the sun setting into the Celtic Sea. Just before it disappeared over the horizon, its top edge burst into a brilliant green light for half a second, then was gone.

Green flash! they'd cried in unison, laughing.

Snap! he'd shouted, hugging her closer...

Gratin Dauphinois for supper, she decided.

She fed Digory and began unpacking the fruit and vegetables. As she sorted and stored them away she was thinking about her last time with Kitto – only five months ago.

She'd heard from Ester that he was living and working in the studio attached to Chykembro, Bethan's house above Lamorna where Ester was living. On the very day Ester moved into Chyangwyns, she saw him strolling around Newlyn fish market and watched him until she began to feel like a stalker. She finally caught his eye and went over to him. They chatted self-consciously about she couldn't remember what. By the time he'd suggested they go for a coffee she'd realised that her desire for him was as strong as ever.

They arranged to spend the night together – which involved her lying to Edward and Ester again. It was just that one final night, and most of the next day, but those twenty-four hours had become a book-marked page in her life, which she returned to again and again.

Nowadays, who did she have in her life? Some acquaintances, neighbours and associates, a few too-distant friends and a couple of too-immediate family members. She enjoyed her own company and could use her solitude creatively. She was never really lonely, although she occasionally missed the ordinary easy intimacy of friendships she'd once taken so much for granted. Sometimes, too, without warning, she would find herself recollecting the extraordinary power of passion.

Tomas appeared in the doorway.

'God, I really slept.'

'Good.'

He watched as she took potatoes from a bag, telling him what she had planned for their meal.

'I'll do the leeks, if you like.'

'Great.'

'I worked in the hotel kitchen last summer.'

He made long lengthwise incisions in the leeks and rinsed them meticulously under the tap.

She stopped peeling the potatoes to pull a large, pink head of garlic from a string of them hanging in the narrow larder and placed it on his cutting board.

'This is home-grown.'

They became absorbed in the preparations for a quarter of an hour. Tomas broke the silence.

'Can I ask you some questions?'

'About...?'

'*Bimarian Ground.*'

'Yes.'

'"Chyangwyns"...'

'In Cornish it means, *the house in the wind.* Appropriate, I suppose.'

He nodded, becoming thoughtful.

'You put it with "Carnmarth". Gave them the title, "Accommodating Sorrow".'

'Carnmarth is another Cornish place name. It means, *horse rock-pile* or cairn. I wrote them after Ebril died and we'd buried her out on the moor with a cairn covering her grave.'

'I thought that's what the poem was about.'

We could go there later, when we walk Digory. It's not far.'

'Yes. I'd like to.'

'I used the word accommodating to mean compliance,

acceptance. They're not unhappy poems.'

'No, they're not. What about "Racing With My Spirit"?'

She found the cheese grater in the back of a drawer.

'Come on, Tomas, you do some digging. What does it say to you?'

Taken aback by her turning the tables on him, he dug deeper into his memory of the poem.

'I imagine you were using the horse as a metaphor, but it's about Ebril as well.'

'Yes.'

He closed his eyes. 'There's the line, "*Snuff out my caution, you quick-shifting spirit –*".'

'God, do you know them all?'

He ignored her question. 'I can see you wanting Ebril's strength to be yours – so that your spirits can race together as equals.'

'That's close enough.'

His questions were stirring up a gamut of feelings. Surely enough time had passed for these poems to not affect her now. But somehow they did.

They worked well together in her over-warm kitchen. By the time she'd grated the cheese and heated the milk everything was ready for assembling in the gratin dish.

'Do you like kasha?' She held up a bag of rust-coloured kernels.

'I've never had it.'

'Roasted buckwheat groats. It has an earthy flavour that goes well with potatoes. We'll have some, shall we?'

Without waiting for a reply she began measuring out the grain.

'What about a salad? There's chicory and watercress. Could you make a dressing?'

'Sure.'

With her encouragement, he opened cupboard doors and peered into the larder, searching for potential ingredients. When he'd found what he wanted he said, 'Ebril meant a lot to you.'

'She still does. We were together for such a long time, something powerful melded between us. Something no one recognised or could even imagine.' She looked at him. 'At least until you came along.'

He flushed and shrugged his shoulders.

'After she was gone I had to work very hard to find that strength in myself, to face some of the challenges that were streaming into my life. I think that was her lasting gift to me.'

She put the dish in the oven and hung her apron inside the cupboard door.

'If all that sounds too fey, just tell me to... '

'No! It doesn't. Really.'

They set the table in the sitting room. Tomas loaded some logs into the stove while Jenna put more fuel into the Rayburn.

She asked him to fetch two stemmed glasses from the dresser and take them into the music room. She brought in a corked wine bottle and placed it on the floor between the two oversized cushions.

'What's this?' he asked, sitting next to her.

'We've got half an hour. I think we deserve an aperitif, don't you?'

She carefully uncorked the bottle and filled the small glasses with a sparkling amber liquid.

'I haven't forgotten the doctor's warning about drinking too much, but this little bit shouldn't hurt.'

'What is it?'

'My father always made his own wines, and mead when he kept bees. This was always my very favourite – quince, from the tree in our orchard. He says it's the most difficult one to get right, because it takes a long time to mature. But when it's ready it has the most wonderful bouquet, and such a delicate flavour.'

She handed him a glassful. 'I want to propose a toast for your birthday tomorrow.'

She held up her glass and waited for him to do the same. 'Wishing you a very memorable day, Tomas. And a fulfilling year ahead.'

They touched glasses and sipped the wine.

Tomas said that he could taste crisp autumn days.

'There's a good third of a haiku in that remark, Tomas. Don't lose it!'

'Okay.'

She could see that he didn't like being teased, even gently.

'What about some music?' she quickly asked. 'Will you choose something?'

They both looked up at the long row of CDs before he went to have a look. There was too much to choose from, most of it unknown to him: quite a few classical chamber pieces, folk and blues, a lot of jazz, world music. He felt uncomfortable, being put on the spot like this, but he persevered, flipping through the cases.

He was about to give up and ask what she'd like to hear when he spotted an image he recognised. It was a Byzantine icon of a Mother and Child on the front of an album of religious songs – sung in Gaelic by Norin Ni Riain. Lorca's aunt had sent him a copy from Ireland. They'd listened to it the one time they'd smoked dope together.

He slipped it into the player, adjusted the volume, and sat back beside her.

'Is this all right?'

'Yes.' She leaned back. 'Just exactly right.'

They listened to Ni Riain's radiant, soaring soprano voice for a quarter of an hour without speaking. By then Tomas was becoming lethargic, so he sat upright, arms hugging his knees.

'I like the humour in "Custodians".'

She looked puzzled.

'In *Bimarian Ground*. The line about "holding onto my wits by its short curly tail". Was it more difficult to write – a lipogram *and* a sonnet?'

'Yes. Very. I meant it as a lighter take on things that are important to me, and the way I try to live. Perseverance, self-reliance, a quiet mind.'

'They're also in "Containing Most Things".'

'Yes. You're right.'

She put a hand to her throat. 'I hadn't realised how many of those poems came out of wanting a peaceful place of my own.'

'Your fogou.'

It felt as though his delving had become a surgeon's knife, moving closer to her heart.

'Isn't that what you said you need sometimes, too, Tomas? A quiet place to complete what's begun.'

He nodded and sipped his wine.

She gazed at him, finding herself unaccountably moved, then had to look away.

'How do you do it, Tomas?'

'What?' He sounded defensive.

'You sit there without the book, discussing my poems as though they were your own. That's not from studying them in class, is it?'

'No, not really.'

There was an emotional stillness between them as they sat in silence again, drinking the wine and listening to the end of the CD. Was it because the unexpected journey they'd taken together over the past two long days was nearing its end? By this time tomorrow Tomas would be out celebrating with his sister and his friend Lorca – and his father? She would be having supper with Edward and Ester, discussing the success of Ester's newly launched women's group, or the progress of Edward's enterprise – opening the house to paying guests just before Easter.

'Shall we eat?'

After they'd brought the food to the table Jenna placed the fat, green candles between their empty glasses and poured them each another half-glassful of the quince wine.

They enjoyed the meal, relaxed and comfortable in each other's company. He told her how much he liked the kasha's nutty taste. She praised the salad dressing he'd concocted, using lime juice and honey – a lovely tang against the chicory's bitter bite.

Their talk ranged around poets and poetry, of course, and the impact of the Celtic landscapes and languages on particular writers and artists. While they were discussing the failure of state education to ignite creative intelligence, Tomas said he had read somewhere that the root of the word education is *to draw out*.

'Yes, it's from the Latin: *educo*.'

'But, wouldn't that mean that everything we need to know is already there inside us? Just waiting? All the teacher would have to do is draw it out.'

He gave a wry laugh.

'That hasn't been your experience, has it?'

'No. For me education's always meant, *to cram in*, and *to suppress*.'

Jenna agreed. 'I have a friend, Nia. In fact I'll be staying with her in Cardiff. She told me that in Welsh there's only one word – *dysgu* – that means both to teach and to learn.'

'That's incredible! I had no idea.'

'So when you asked me yesterday if I'd ever taught... '

'Did I?'

'You did. And, if we'd been speaking Welsh, I could have said, "Yes, I'm learning all the time".'

He laughed again.

They got through second helpings, and when the meal was nearly over Tomas asked, 'Can I say something about just one more poem?'

Like a child, she thought, asking for another sweet.

'All right, one more then.'

'"Withholding Light"?'

'Go on.'

'It's such an affirming poem. Or is it "confirming"? Anyway, it really affected me when I first read it.'

'Did it?'

'You probably never saw the Disney film, *Beauty and the Beast*, but there's this scene near the end, when the beast is dying and Beauty tells him that she loves him. When she kisses him he becomes... *transformed*. He's this massive great hulk of a beast, and he slowly rises up off the ground, floating in the air, swaying and turning like he's under water. And then out of his paws come these brilliant rays of light – like laser beams – shooting out in all directions, while his paws turn into human hands and feet, and he becomes the handsome young prince he used to be.'

'That sounds amazing.'

She cherished his innocence. Fleetingly, she imagined him as a child coming home from the cinema, sitting at the kitchen table and describing this scene to his mother just as he had to her. That dreary room would have been much brighter and warmer then.

'But... why did I tell you that? I can't... '

He paused, frowning, shaking his head.

Jenna wondered if he could be tipsy on two small glasses of wine. She didn't know if he ever drank alcohol, and she began feeling anxious and responsible. Whatever was she thinking, offering him alcohol after such a traumatic day? Two days!

'No, wait. I've got it!'

He held up one finger and closed his eyes, smiling, pleased with himself.

'"Withholding Light". That was the image I had when I first read "Withholding Light".'

'Was it?'

He was relaxed and spontaneous and had been in such good humour since he woke from his nap. She shouldn't keep being so critical of herself.

'It's as though you were saying that we have an obligation to live our lives *fully*,' he was saying. 'To be ourselves, and to... to let our light and our beauty shine out. Especially for the people we love. And if that light's held back – not *drawn out* – it can deform us. It might even destroy us.'

Out of nowhere, like a thunder cloud looming, threatening to darken all her pleasure in this evening, she couldn't stop her thoughts.

Who does my light shine out for now? How fully alive am I in this solitary life? And then a remorseful self-judgement: *Dear God, what compromises have I made?*

Who were her kindred spirits? She didn't have any now. And no one filled that tender space meant for love in her life any more. In which case, *of course* she was lonely. She'd better face it, before she too became transformed – into a cranky, middle-aged recluse.

THIRTEEN

They were sitting by the stove with mugs of decaf coffee. Digory seemed to sense Jenna's subdued spirits. Whining, he stood with his front paws on her knees, then he went over to the Welsh dresser, sniffing the air and whining again.

Jenna got up and took a brown egg from the top dresser shelf.

'What's going on?' Tomas asked.

Digory was tense with excitement. When he saw the egg he jumped up, all four feet off the ground.

'He wants to play with Peggy.'

'Peggy?'

She held the egg between her thumb and index finger to show him.

'He's never been keen on toys, except for Peggy.'

She stood by the window while Digory moved into position, alert and expectant.

'He invented this game for himself, years ago.'

She bent forward, holding the egg in the cup of one hand, and bowled it down the corridor.

Tomas laughed as the solid rubber toy bounced high, veered in one direction then another, hitting the wall on the second bounce and continuing on an unpredictable course, with Digory chasing after it. He stopped it with a pat of one paw before it reached the kitchen and carried it back to the dresser.

'Now I'm redundant.' She sat again.

Digory dropped the egg in front of the dresser and quickly cocked his head back to watch it bounce. He picked it up and charily dropped it again. On the third attempt it landed awkwardly and rolled under the dresser. He lay flat, head on the floor, peering through the narrow gap. A paw shot under to retrieve the toy, and when he had it in his mouth he started again. Whenever he wasn't able to paw it towards him, he'd push it further underneath, then race round behind the dresser to fetch it.

'What happens if it ends up in the middle and he can't reach it?'

'I keep a bamboo stick in the corner to rake it out with, but it doesn't happen often. He's honed his skills into a fine art over the years.'

They continued watching Digory at his game.

'How old is he?'

'Mmm... seven, I think. He was Father's dog. I've only had him with me since he left Hendra.'

Tomas looked thoughtful. 'So Digory taught himself the game at Hendra?'

'That's right.'

'With the dresser?'

'Yes. Oh, I see what you're thinking. Most of the furniture here – all the old pieces – came from Hendra. Father didn't want anything when we left the farm, so Ester and I brought everything to Chyangwyns. It's such a big house, Edward and I never had enough furniture for all the rooms. When I knew I was moving to The

Fogou I claimed the pieces that I've always liked and brought them over, one by one. Some days I felt like a child furnishing a doll's house.'

'How did you come to be living at Chyangwyns in the first place?'

She hesitated. 'It's a long story.'

'That's all right. But if you don't want to... '

'No, the short of it is that Chyangwyns belonged to Edward's grandparents, and when they died it was left to Edward's father. He was an officer in the Royal Navy and thought farming was beneath him – and the role of country squire beyond him. So he decided to auction it off – the farm, livestock, machinery, furniture and all – much to the chagrin of the locals.

'Edward and his older brother, Philip, were both in the navy as well. When Philip was killed in the Falklands War, Edward got out as soon as he could, on medical grounds. He eventually had his brother's share of their grandparents' inheritance as well as his own, and decided that he wanted Chyangwyns.'

'So, it wasn't auctioned.'

'Yes, it was! His father wanted to dispose of everything quickly, and there were on-going wrangles between the two of them over it. When Edward turned up at the auction his father was furious.

'The furnishings went first, then some small parcels of land just outside the estate. When bidding started on the livestock Edward joined in. He managed to buy the lot, which surprised everyone. The herd didn't go cheaply. Then he secured most of the machinery and other farm equipment for a fair price. All that remained was the farm itself, and the house with its ten acres of parkland.

'What happened then was extraordinary. The locals all

knew the Mundeys and realised that, without property of his own, if Edward didn't succeed in buying the farm he wouldn't have anywhere to put everything he'd already bought.'

'They wanted him to have it.'

'Yes. So they hardly bid against him at all. He got the farm for a very reasonable price.'

'That's wonderful.'

'Bidding on the house started off slow, until his father stunned the locals by getting his wife to bid against Edward – to increase their takings. Everyone else withdrew, and when she realised how exposed she was – bidding against her step-son on a property they'd never wanted – she pulled out as well. Edward got Chyangwyns for the lowest reserve price, unchallenged.'

'What an amazing story.'

'My father was there at the auction. He said that when it was over the crowd wouldn't leave, because they wanted to celebrate Edward's success and their own part in it. His parents went off without speaking to him, and I don't think they ever did again. Edward became a local hero that day. To me as well.'

'Some of that's in the "Proportions" sonnets, in your *Selected Verses*, isn't it?'

Jenna blanched, remembering those youthful poems, describing how she had come to love this older, worldly man who courted her. Some of the third sonnet was too close to the voice Shakespeare had given to Othello, speaking about his Desdemona:

> *She loved me for the dangers I had passed,*
> *and I loved her that she did pity them.*

She hadn't been conscious of it at the time, but those echoing lines were there, and she'd come to dislike the whole of "Proportions" because of them. If there were ever another edition of *Selected Verses* published it certainly wouldn't include those sonnets.

Digory's game was over. He made his way to the kitchen for a drink of water.

Tomas suddenly noticed the empty space where Kitto's painting had hung. He looked at Jenna.

'Sancreed Beacon is in your... in the guest room. I haven't finished in there yet.' She got up and he followed her.

He unfolded the sheet hanging on the rug rail and began making up the bed. Together, they managed to get the four corners of the duvet into its cover.

'I know I have no right to ask... '

'Go on.'

'I've been wondering why you're living here in the stables.'

'I'm sure you must have been.'

She fluffed up the duvet and spread it over the bed.

Almost without realising she was saying it, she went on. 'Edward and I have had problems, as you know.'

Tomas said nothing.

'A few years ago, when the foot and mouth plague loomed and then ravaged through the farm, Edward's depression deepened. He took the decision to give up farming, which was realistic under the circumstances. But once he'd done that and didn't feel any better, he began talking about pushing further out – selling up and leaving Cornwall. Making a fresh start somewhere else.'

'And you couldn't do that.'

'I didn't see it as any kind of solution to our problems.'

She excused herself and went to the kitchen. She lifted

a basket from the larder floor and rummaged through it. She laid a tack hammer and a jar full of nails on the counter, turned and leant back against it.

Why was she doing this – disclosing her personal life? She'd fallen into a confessional mode so easily, as though she'd been living alone here for months rather than days, ruminating over the past. She wasn't blaming Tomas, who was naturally inquisitive. He'd been so perceptive – or was it receptive – this evening.

Digory came and sat, staring at her.

'Please don't look at me like that,' she told him. She picked up the hammer and jar and returned to the guest room.

With each of them holding a side of the painting, they positioned it against the back wall, over the verse.

Tomas shook his head.

They lifted it above the poem, then a bit higher.

'Here?'

He nodded and held onto the canvas while Jenna stepped back to look.

'Yes, that'll do.'

She hammered the nails into a seam of lime mortar in the stone wall and they lowered the frame over them.

She folded back the duvet and sat on the futon. Tomas perched on the stool. He followed her gaze to the painting.

'A year ago last Easter I decided to ride Ebril up there.' She pointed to the top of Sancreed Beacon.

'We usually kept to our side of the moor. There was never any need to cross the lane. But a trek up to the Beacon was always Ebril's favourite, so I gave in to her once in a while.

'It was raining, and a minibus full of holidaymakers

127

came around the curve going much too fast. Instead of braking hard, the driver sounded his horn and Ebril bolted and tried to leap over the hedge bank. She skidded and fell back, breaking her leg. She was in agony.

'I called Edward, and when he came racing down with his shotgun the young people in the van thought he was going to shoot them.'

'God.'

'It was a nightmare.'

Tomas struggled not to say how sorry he was.

'I'd fractured an arm and my collarbone, and they wouldn't heal. So I was disabled, mourning for my Ebril, and not getting much support – because Edward was struggling with his own illness and anger.'

'So, that's when you...'

'At that point we could have gone our separate ways. I could have left Chyangwyns and Edward and gone for good. Instead, I went to stay with Father and Ester at Hendra, hoping I could mend there – physically and emotionally.

'But then we had to find somewhere for Father to live, and sell Hendra – the place where my heart had always lived, and that I loved very deeply.'

Tomas shook his head.

'By then I'd realised that I couldn't write. Not a word or a letter. Nothing. I couldn't even read.'

She glanced at Tomas. When he raised his head she saw pain in his eyes.

He said, 'That must have been...'

'I half expected I'd end up crawling off somewhere to die. Instead, I had...'

She looked down at her hands, folded in her lap, then at Tomas.

' ...I had a change of heart and went back to Edward.'

Digory wandered into the room and was sniffing the futon. When she saw that he was about to pee on it she shouted, 'Don't you dare! Come on, you.'

She took him into the yard and stayed with him, then escorted him back to the sitting room. Tomas stood with his back to the stove.

'I couldn't leave him out there on his own,' she told him. 'If he wanders over to the house I'll be in serious trouble.'

Tomas wondered if she was joking.

She gave Digory a pat on his ribs. 'Good boy. Come get a biscuit.'

She went through the conservatory, Digory beside her. He was making a series of graceful leaps.

When she returned Tomas asked, 'Do we get biscuits, too?'

She lifted down the heart-shaped box and peered inside. 'There's only one each, I'm afraid.'

She held the box open for him to choose, then took the last one for herself.

Tomas concentrated very hard on folding the biscuit paper into smaller and smaller squares.

'You were telling me how you ended up living here.'

'I was, wasn't I?'

She sounded diffident, stifling a yawn.

'Come on, Tomas, we've still got work to do.'

He opted to do the washing-up. She dried and put things away.

'Ester offered to move into The Fogou when it was ready,' she explained.

'I can't imagine her here. I mean... '

They caught each other's eye and both smiled.

'Neither can I. If I'd agreed to that, I'd have given up

the only place where I could write again, which was more important to me than anything else.'

'Yes.'

'Do you remember my poem, "Lost and Found"?'

His eyes scanned the ceiling, the lime-washed spaces between black beams.

'You said: *poetry is the breath of the soul.*'

She nodded.

'It is. For *me* it is. And that's what I needed – to breathe again. Edward and Ester had become companions, and that convinced me it was right to come here.'

They were both looking around the sitting room, but seeing different aspects.

'The building work dragged on for such a long time. I started bringing my furnishings over – more of my books, some personal belongings – spending part of each day here, trying to write and then actually managing to write. Almost at once I began writing the lipograms.'

'You wrote them here?'

She nodded again.

'At first it was literally playing a game. I'd tried other forms and constraints, but none of them seemed to offer me a way back, so I experimented with the lipogram – without the letter "e". I started with something apparently simple – like one of Charles Causley's children's rhymes. When I'd managed two lines fairly easily I felt very pleased with myself:

> *As if by magic I can calm this storm.*
> *I'll chant a drowning boson's song I know...*

She put the tea towel on the drying rail and watched him as he wiped down the counter.

'You must be exhausted.'

'Not really.' He looked at his watch. 'It's only nine o'clock. You wanted to do some preparation for your Cardiff reading.'

'Let's take Digory for his walk first. See what we feel like when we get back.'

FOURTEEN

Tomas followed Jenna up the track onto the moor. Although the night was cold, he felt the freshness in the air rather than its chill.

A flash of headlights behind them made him turn to look.

'That'll be Ester,' she told him. 'Back from her supervision group.'

The moon had risen over the moorland, giving a strong direct light as well as illuminating the broad bank of clouds racing beneath it. He found himself silently reciting a couplet from Jenna's *Selected Verses*:

> *The fierce full moon is marking time tonight,*
> *etching the frosted fields a deeper white.*

Where the track petered out they kept to a narrow path that threaded through the bracken, winding between moor stones. They hadn't brought a torch with them, but she could find her way there with her eyes closed.

Digory made great swirling forays among the low shadows – away from them, then back again. Tomas saw the cairn profiled on the horizon: a dark mound rising above clumps of gorse and outcrops of stone.

They turned onto another path and soon came to Carnmarth, Ebril's grave. He stood close beside her. Digory stopped his cavorting and sat.

'*April, my goblin...* ' she whispered.

He wanted to whisper the rest of the line, but it didn't feel appropriate. After another minute she led them onto a less worn path.

'Stay close behind me, Tomas,' she told him, putting her left hand behind her. 'There are some stony outcrops along here and I don't want you tripping up.'

He tentatively took her hand and held onto it until they arrived at a flat, open clearing. They paused to look up at the moon, which was edging the clouds with rainbows.

Jenna could sense something in his silence. 'Wishing upon a star?'

He shook his head.

'Tell me.'

'What?'

'What you're thinking.'

She waited.

The dark silence of the moor made him braver. 'I was thinking about the poems at the end of *Bimarian Ground*. "Six Ways of Living".'

'Were you?' She thought she knew why.

'I've wondered what makes them different from the others. I guess it's because they're more... there's more passion in them. They seem more... personal, and you can tell that they're true. Lorca says they're like confessional poems.'

She laughed. 'Is that what you've been wondering? Am I turning into a confessional poet, like Sharon Olds – "the *connoisseuse* of slugs"?'

'I don't know Sharon Olds.' He sounded embarrassed.

'That's probably just as well.'

'Okay.'

They both fell into a long silence.

She stepped onto the path that turned toward Chyan-gwyns and he followed.

Winding their way back, the skeletal fronds of last year's bracken brushed uncomfortably against her legs.

'Anyway, I don't think poets can ever tell the whole truth about themselves,' she said finally, 'any more than anyone else can. We don't *know* the whole truth, do we? If we did we'd be enlightened – free of all the constraints life demands of us. And we probably wouldn't be writing poems about it!'

He stopped walking.

'But isn't that why we write them? Trying to reach what we half know is there, even if we can't get there? Writing for ourselves first of all – that's what I do – and then for whoever else might want to understand.'

His directness and his insight into what they both struggled for astounded her. She felt chastened by him.

'Yes. Yes, you're right, Tomas.'

They walked on towards the farm track.

'I suppose those six poems were written as a kind of... purge.'

'Purge?'

'When I came back here from Hendra, to Edward, I felt guilty and responsible for most of our problems. I made up my mind to be more open and honest with him, so that we could make a fresh start. And I tried. I did *try*, but it was too much to achieve on my own.'

She could see lights burning in Edward's bedroom, and now one was switched on in Ester's room.

'I guess I was hoping that Edward would be one of those who, as you said, "might want to understand". But Edward doesn't read my poems these days. He used to, privately, but even then he hardly spoke to me about them.'

'He hasn't read "My Quick Flight"?'

She gave an ironic laugh.

'No, Tomas.'

'You've published a poem about a relationship your husband doesn't even know about? Or does he?'

They went through the back gate at Chyangwyns.

'Perhaps he doesn't want to know.'

'I should read those poems again.'

Sensor lights flashed on as they approached the two hen houses.

'If you do,' she said, looking directly into his eyes, 'try to keep in mind what attracted you to them in the first place, okay? Every poem has to stand on its own – with nothing more to enlighten it than the page it's printed on.'

'Yes.'

Jenna walked on ahead.

'I want to make sure the hens are closed up. Not that I don't trust Edward, exactly.'

She checked that all the doors and latches were secure, then opened one of a row of nesting boxes and felt inside. The eggs hadn't been collected.

'Damn! Take these, will you?'

One by one, she handed him the eggs.

A hen sleeping in one of the boxes let out a clucking complaint as she opened the second hatch.

Reaching for another egg Tomas nearly dropped them all, so he began filling his coat pockets with them.

As they started back to The Fogou, he unbuttoned his coat and held it away from his sides to keep the eggs from knocking together.

Jenna took an empty basket from the kitchen cupboard and held it out while Tomas emptied his pockets.

He looked at his watch: ten o'clock.

'You ready for bed?' she asked.

'No, not yet.'

FIFTEEN

Tomas carried one of the wooden chairs from the sitting room into the library. Jenna sat at her writing table, where a dozen books she'd taken from her shelves lay in piles around the oil lamp. Her worn leather notebook was open to a blank page and she was writing into it.

'It's too late to be doing this.'

He was tired now, but said nothing and was trying not to show it.

'Which of the poems I read at Exeter do you remember best?'

He sat next to her. 'Your poems?'

'Other than mine.'

He thought for a moment.

'There were lots, but two or three were... wait a minute.'

He came back, turning the pages of his own notebook.

'I made a list of the ones I wanted to read again, and some of the books I wanted to find in the library.'

He drew his finger down a page filled with columns.

'I managed to get a few from the library, but most of the others were out of print, or they haven't been published in Britain.'

'For instance?'

'Gillian Clarke?'

'She's certainly in print. Who else?'

'Denise Levertov. You read two of hers – one right after the other.'

'Yes.' She smiled. 'It doesn't surprise me that you like her poetry, Tomas.'

'Why?'

'I'm not sure. Something to do with her "pilgriming spirit", probably.'

'I don't know many American poets.'

'It depends on what you mean by "American". Levertov was born in Essex.'

'Was she?'

'Her mother was Welsh and her father was a Russian Hassidic Jew. He emigrated to England and became an Anglican priest. After Denise moved to the United States she developed an interest in eastern mysticism. Then she became a Roman Catholic before she died.'

'A pilgriming spirit,' he repeated. 'I really liked the ones you read.'

'Yes, they're lovely – so many of them are. I feel a real link between the way she wrote about her life and what I struggle for in my own poems.'

She got up and took a paperback from a shelf.

'I was sent this copy of her *New Selected Poems* to review before it was published here. Reviews don't pay much, but I get to keep the books!'

She held it out to him. 'You can have this one, Tomas.'

He kept his hands on the table. 'Oh! No, I couldn't… '

'I'd like you to have it.'

He didn't move.

She went back to the shelf and returned with an identical copy.

'Look. I was given this one as a birthday present from my editor. Pam doesn't read my reviews, apparently. So I think you were meant to have that copy, Tomas.'

He took the book and opened it. There were pencilled notes written in the margins of some of the pages, making it even more precious to him.

'This is wonderful. Thank you so much.'

'You're very welcome. I can imagine you writing poetry reviews yourself one day.'

'I don't think so.'

He placed the book squarely in front of him, then picked up the notebook, turning pages until he found what he was looking for.

'I wanted to ask you about the first one you read. It begins:

> *Fully occupied with growing – that's*
> *the amaryllis. Growing especially*
> *at night...*

But I can't remember the title.'

He offered her his notebook, holding it open across the table.

She hesitated for only a second, but he noticed. 'Take it,' he insisted.

She took it and looked at the lines. 'It's called, "The Métier of Blossoming". Probably her very last poem.'

'The other one you read was... ' He consulted his notebook. '"The Disclosure"?'

'That's right:

> *From the shrivelling gray*
> *silk of its cocoon,*

a creature slowly
is pushing out
to stand clear... '

Her phone began ringing, inside her handbag in the bedroom. They looked at each other before she got up to answer it.

He sat motionless, listening.

'Hello. Yes, that's right. Yes, he's here. Would you like to speak with him? Hold on.'

She reappeared and handed the phone to him.

'Take it to the sitting room,' she whispered.

Tomas carried it through and sat in his chair by the stove. He held the phone in both hands for nearly a minute, took a deep breath, then lifted it to his ear.

'Hello?'

'Tom?' said his father's voice. 'What the fuck are you playing at?'

A quarter of an hour had passed and Tomas still sat, considering what he should tell Jenna and what he wanted to tell her, which were not exactly the same thing. She'd been so open with him. He knew he should confide in her, but it was late – much too late, he decided. And he didn't want to become even more of an emotional burden to her than he'd been already.

But there was another reason why he hadn't offered more than a glimpse of his personal life: his long-standing habit of self-protectiveness. Sometimes Tamsyn and Lorca would become exasperated with him over his bloody defensiveness. It must have served some purpose when he was young, but during his adolescence it had armoured itself onto his character to such a degree that he'd begun to see it as a disability. Nowadays he could too easily hide his feelings behind civility and a certain amount of intellectualising, neither of which did him any justice.

When he was feeling positive he could see this as a habit, nothing more. With enough determination – and with practice – he could probably change. At least he hoped he could.

He closed the phone.

The soft light from the oil lamp, shining through the open library doorway and reflecting on the glass, gave the conservatory an ethereal look. He could hear faint music, which Jenna must have put on to give him more privacy while he was speaking with his father. It was a duet for oboe and harpsichord. He'd never heard it before, but he recognised the yearning and the sadness it was describing.

The scent of trumpet lilies caught at the back of his throat. The look of them, standing tall in a wooden half-barrel, their waxy flowers glowing an eerie, glistening white, combined with the music to remind him of the horrendous funeral.

Father, leaning forward onto the empty chair in front of him during the service, his face buried in his folded arms, his half-smothered bass sobs. Tamsyn, a hand on Father's shoulder, looking anxiously at Tomas, who was struggling to breathe through the tight ball in his chest – afraid to let go, but unable to hold back. He felt as if he were trapped in a sealed container that held only raw, bitter grief and a smothering, ghostly nothingness. He'd staggered to his feet as the curtain closed in front of the coffin, holding his breath, trembling until an inner dark-ness came and took him away to somewhere safer.

He went into the library, put the phone on the table and sat beside Jenna.

'That was my father.'

'Yes, I thought it was.'

When she turned a page in her notebook he realised that she wasn't going to ask him about their conversation.

He picked up a book from the top of a pile. Opening it to a book-marked page, he read:

> *To be alive is power,*
> *Existence in itself,*
> *Without a further function,*
> *Omnipotence enough.*

He hadn't read many of Emily Dickinson's poems, but he knew that she'd lived a reclusive spinster's life in New England, and that virtually none of the thousands of verses she'd written had been published during her lifetime.

He closed the book and put it back on the pile, wondering if he would meet a similar fate.

'She wrote a lot of poems full of painful self-disclosure, but I'm only going to read a few of the lighter ones.' She turned to another page in her notebook. 'Most of them are short and pithy:

> *To see the Summer Sky*
> *Is Poetry, though never in a Book it lie—*
> *True Poems flee— .'*

He was hardly listening.

'She could have written "fly" rather than "flee" – to complete the rhyme. I'm sure Pam would have picked up on that one straightaway. But, if she'd wanted "fly" she would have written "fly", bless her.'

'He doesn't want me to come home.'

She looked up in alarm.

'What! Not at all?'

'I don't know. Not now, anyway. Not tomorrow.'

'Dear God!' She put a hand over his.

'He might change his mind when Tamsyn's back. She told him she'd only come home if he agreed to stop drinking. My sister's very strong-willed, so he'll know she means it. It's the best thing that could happen, really.'

'But... where will you go, Tomas?'

'I can stay with my grandparents at Newlyn for a while. That's where Tamsyn's been living. We'll do another swap.'

'I thought your sister was living with her boyfriend.'

He gave her a penetrating stare and pulled his hand away. It was obvious that she hadn't meant to say this.

'Who told you that?'

She looked mortified. 'I... it was Ester. She spoke with Arthur. Dr Sanders. He phoned her first thing this morning to let us know he'd be at the hospital when we got there.'

Tomas continued staring at her.

'He told her he'd met you and your family during your mother's illness. And that your father had been depressed over your mother's death.'

'He was depressed *long* before that! What else did he tell her?'

'Nothing! Nothing, really. Just that your sister was... '

'Did he tell her that my father's an alcoholic? And that I'm queer? And that my sister was shacked up with... '

'No! Stop it, Tomas!'

She reached out her hand, but he drew back and stood

up. He stared for a few seconds longer, then quickly grabbed his notebook, stormed down to the guest room and slammed the door.

SIXTEEN

Tomas threw himself down on the futon, unable to catch his breath. Digory was barking. He heard Jenna go to the sitting room to reassure him, speaking in a calm voice. He held his head in his hands, feeling a deep sadness beginning to rise up. He tried to stop it by keeping his anger there in his chest, but then his mind began racing. He would have to get out of here. Walk away – run away. He looked at his watch: just past eleven o'clock. He couldn't go home – and not to Newlyn, because Tamsyn was still there.

If only he could get to Exeter. He had money, but there wouldn't be another train tonight, and anyway Lorca would be home tomorrow. He wondered if he should phone for a taxi to take him to a hotel somewhere – anywhere. There were plenty of them standing half-empty in winter. But he didn't have a mobile phone. And besides, he didn't want to be anywhere no one would be able to find him.

This thought worried him. He lay back on the bed, his arms over his eyes. Of course he would have to stay here. If he didn't get some sleep tonight he would be ill again.

He had no right to blame Jenna for knowing those

things about him. What did it matter now anyway? He felt a deep remorse over his outburst. He should go and apologise, so they could begin to feel safe with each other again. But he was so tired. Exhausted.

There was no way to hold back now. His sadness was going to find a way out whether he wanted it to or not.

He cried quietly at first, then openly, sobbing long, deep sobs until the worst of it had spent itself. He took a handkerchief from his pocket, dried his eyes and face, then tucked it under the pillow.

The light in the library glowed above the guest room partition, but the music had stopped. In fact The Fogou was completely still. He looked up at the open skylight and listened. There was no wind, no sound at all.

He hadn't realised until now that he was missing the sound of the sea. Wherever he was in West Penwith he always believed or imagined that he could hear it, coming in from the English Channel or from the Celtic Sea. But this place, midway between the two, seemed ringed with silence.

The stillness lulled him, and he began thinking about his mother's parents, Jory the fisherman and Gram Wenna: the Sunday afternoon family visits to their cottage on the hill at Newlyn, and the occasional summer holidays he spent with them there.

They had come to Lamorna almost every afternoon or evening, sometimes both, during those last weeks when his mother was still at home. Before they left, while Grampa was invariably in the living room with his father, talking about the past, or politics, or whatever else they might find to disagree about, Gram would come up to his room, sit by the window, fold her hands in her lap and say, 'Now, Heyjyk,' – she always called him her duckling

– 'tell me three things about your day'. It was an odd thing to ask, but he understood what she really meant: *I know that you have a life of your own somewhere in all this. I haven't forgotten you.*

He could always find three things to tell her, even if they were only about doing the cooking with Tamsyn, spotting an unusual sea bird preening on the quay, or sitting with his mother, sometimes reading a poem to her from his notebook. Toward the end he would occasionally read one of his own, supposing that she didn't suspect he'd written it. But on the day before she went to the hospice she whispered, 'Read me that one about the brook again, Tomas. Our little stream running down through the woods.' It was the only time she'd asked to hear a poem again. When he'd finished reciting it she smiled and closed her eyes.

'Come and visit me, Heyjyk,' Gram would say before getting up to leave. He knew he was her favourite.

He went and got the crumpled sheet of paper from the folder in his rucksack. He copied the two lines of yesterday's poem into his notebook, as he always did. Reading the couplet, he was satisfied enough with the first line:

> *You watch, dumb, as your past slinks forward*
> *to find you...*

But was the second line too final?

> *Nothing can stop this chopping of blood*
> *knots that bind you.*

He wondered if the line should begin more tentatively –

Can nothing stop? But that would disrupt the meter. *Chopping* was such a violent word; should it be *slicing* or *cutting* of blood knots? No, too weak. *Untying*? Too passive – and too many syllables. Anyway, it felt and sounded right when it had come to him at the well. Starting to fiddle about with it now, instead of thinking about the twelve lines that should come before, was just an avoidance. In fact, trying to do anything at this moment felt like an avoidance.

After Tomas had slammed out of the room and she'd settled Digory, it was impossible for Jenna to concentrate on anything.

She couldn't decide whether to go to him or not. Surely she shouldn't become even more involved in all this now. If she did, she might end up mothering him, which would be painful for both of them. At his age, he should be moving out of his parents' shadows and finding the emotional support he needed from his peers. But then, wasn't Tomas more sensitive, less confident and mature than most other boys his age? There was also the added burden of his emerging sexual identity. He was being thwarted by his father, and at the same time trying to come to terms with the loss of his mother. And now this injury – whatever might have caused it. So much pain. No wonder he became angry and sullen, mistrustful at times.

She could remember herself at his age. It hadn't been an easy time for her either. There was the cavernous hole that her mother's sudden death had left in the middle of her heart. Mother had always been her support, offering understanding and encouragement all through her adolescence.

'You have such a way with words, Jenna,' she would tell her. And, 'Good things are sure to come to you in time, my darling.'

Father had retreated into the routine of farm work and his garden, doggedly carrying on as usual and expecting his girls to do the same. Ester secured a place at university and seemed to move on quickly and easily, but despite their differences, Ester's departure that autumn had been another painful loss. With just the two of them at home, Father had been harder to please. Ester always seemed to be able to manage it.

The only time she remembered impressing Father enough for him to hug her tightly against him was when she brought Edward home – to tell him they were engaged to be married. *As though he were a prize bull,* she thought, and then was appalled at having thought it.

As for Tomas, the hard truth was that whatever sympathy and concern she felt for him and his situation tonight, he would have to carry it all away with him tomorrow. And being honest with herself, she didn't think she had much left to give him. Hardly any sleep last night, today an emotional helter-skelter, and now this.

She opened an anthology of poetry, read through the entire table of contents, then closed it again. Turning down the oil lamp and looking above the partition, she could see light in the guest room.

How had their lives become so snagged upon each other's? It would seem incongruous to an outsider that she, now 'thirty-seven in the shade' and still struggling with her own complicated relationships, should find herself so involved in the life of a college boy she hardly knew.

And yet, she could see similarities between herself

and Tomas. Each of them felt close to the mysterious granite-strewn landscapes and covert ancient sites scattered everywhere around West Penwith – fuelling their imaginations and inspiring them. Also, it seemed to her that they were both over-protective of their inner worlds. In different ways they were too introspective for their own good and, she suspected, too constrained by the judgments of others.

Loving can be the most difficult constraint of all, she thought.

SEVENTEEN

Jenna found herself in the kitchen, staring unfocused at the stack of unopened mail lying on the counter. She stood there for several minutes before going down the hallway and knocking at the guest room door.

As she came in, Tomas slipped a sheet of paper into his notebook, then tossed it onto the bedside stool and stretched out on top of the duvet. He was wearing the nightshirt again.

She picked up the notebook and sat, holding it tightly.

'Remember,' she said gently, 'there's no saying sorry.'

He nodded.

'I want to tell you something.'

Again he nodded, watching her.

'I was very impressed by the verse you wrote. They're compelling, confident lines, drawn from strong feelings, which every poet needs. Even if those feelings are painful ones.'

He laid back, hands folded over his chest, looking up at the skylight.

'I'd like to know what's causing you so much pain, because I've come to care for you, Tomas, but I know I have no right to ask.'

When she held out the notebook, he took it and held it tight. Neither of them spoke for several minutes. She felt secure enough in this silence, which was not hers to break.

Tomas sighed.

'Last night – I mean Saturday night – my father started drinking again. I knew he'd already had something before he got home. His face was red and puffy, the way it gets when he drinks red wine. He was bad-tempered and wouldn't even eat the meal I'd made for us. He sat in front of the television watching some stupid programme, the volume turned up really loud, not saying anything. I couldn't wait to finish my supper and go up to my room – to get out of his way. Maybe that's what he wanted, too.

'While I was up there, trying to finish writing something, he drank some rum. I could smell it on his breath when he came into my room.'

'Is that why your sister went to live with her boyfriend?' she asked. 'His drinking?'

'Yes, and he stopped after that – because I told him I'd go too if he didn't. I think he can stop whenever he wants to. But even when he isn't drinking there are a lot of things that get him going. At me, I mean.'

'Because you're the only one left.'

He sat up and put the notebook on the floor between them.

'He spends a lot of time at work, which is good, and there's a member of staff there, Allyson, who he stays with overnight sometimes. The trouble starts when it's just the two of us at home together. He begins picking holes in me and ends up rubbishing me if I don't stay out of his way, which isn't always easy.'

'Rubbishing you?'

'Anything that's different from what *he* thinks is rubbish. Poetry's rubbish. Lorca's rubbish. He blames Lorca for breaking up his little family, which is stupid. Our family fell apart when my mum died. But he thinks Lorca took Tamsyn away. And now maybe me.'

Lorca? She tried to make sense of this, and then she did.

Of course! Lorca is Tamsyn's boyfriend.

'He'd had too much to drink and he began making threats. He told me that he'd been in my room that morning, going through my things, reading Lorca's letters. But I already knew that.'

Tomas closed his eyes and shook his head.

'He accused us of everything filthy and disgusting he could think of. He threatened to give up the cottage – said there's a hotel in Penzance that would give him a job with accommodation just like that. No problem. And I'd have to go fend for myself if I didn't sort myself out. Emotional blackmail.'

'Do you think...?' she hesitated. 'Maybe it's got to happen that way.'

'No! I know what would happen. If he's alone he'll be drinking, and then he'll get the sack and be out on the street. I can't let that happen!'

'You can't stop it, either. Not if he's... '

'I know I can't! And I can't stay living there with him the way things are. I told him that if he carried on drinking I'd really go this time. But, if he stopped I'd stay until I left for university in the autumn.'

'What did he say to that?'

'"Piss off then, if you're going anyway!" And that he wouldn't be buying me some poncey motorbike so I could go swanning off to my faggot friends whenever I fancied.'

'Maybe he felt he'd backed himself into a corner.'

He glowered at her. 'Whose side are you on?'

'I'm not on his side, Tomas! I'm just trying to understand both sides of your situation.'

He swung his legs over the side of the bed.

'Where are you going?'

'To get a drink of water.'

She watched him standing at the pine chest, his back to her, pouring water into the glass.

'Would you like something hot to drink?'

'No, thank you.'

There was a hardness in his voice that disheartened her.

He put the glass on the floor and lay back on the bed.

'I thought, from your phone calls earlier, things were working out for you.'

'So did I.'

He put an arm over his eyes.

'He can't face me, not with Tamsyn coming home. Maybe he's afraid I'll tell her what's happened – or that I already have – which is stupid. All she knows is that he's being bloody unreasonable and I can't take any more of it.'

'There's something else.'

He remained motionless, except for the steady rise and fall of his chest.

'Can you tell me, Tomas?'

He let his arm drop and opened his eyes.

'He had my notebook. It's got my poems in it, and all the ones I've copied out of books. He took it from my room while I was in the bath. He was really drunk and came staggering into the bathroom, laughing.

'He sat down on the edge of the bath and started reading some of the poems in a flowery voice, making fun of them. But they weren't my poems. They were Edward Thomas, Charles Causley, Edwin Morgan... Seamus Heaney, for Christ's sake!

'It was so... ridiculous! I started laughing, too – at him. He was being so pathetic. But that got him angrier and he started shouting at me, telling me to shut the fuck up and calling me all those names again!'

As he was telling her this Tomas' voice grew louder, his speech faster. His hands were clenched and his feet pressed and rubbed against each other. Then he stopped.

Jenna sat motionless and wouldn't look at him – not wanting to distract him. They both waited, wrestling with their own thoughts. Finally, it was hearing the distant call of the tawny owl that eased some of the tension in the room.

'When I stood up in the bath to grab my notebook he pushed me away. I slipped and fell back and bashed my head against the water tap. It was bleeding a lot. My dad turned white. He started gagging, then he bent over and vomited into the bath. When he got up, seeing me sitting there in a bathtub full of blood and sick, he just froze. His face crumpled up and he started crying. Once he gets started he can't stop, so I shouted at him to get out, go away and leave me alone. He just... walked out. Left the house. Probably went to stay with Allyson. He was so pissed, I can't believe he could have driven there. I hope not.'

'Oh, Tomas,' she whispered.

'I don't remember what happened after that. I woke up in my bed.'

He seemed calm, almost reflective now. She couldn't understand how he could manage it. A good deal of practice, she supposed.

'I'll go stay with my grandparents for a while. I've got some money saved from working at the hotel last summer. Lorca wants me to go back to Exeter with him, but I told him that wouldn't work. I've got to stay on at college. If I don't pass my exams I won't be going anywhere!'

'Do you think it's possible that your father came back, or that he didn't leave the house at all?'

He looked at her in disbelief, started to say something, then turned his head away.

'When you woke up this morning, how much could you remember about last night? What you were saying and doing when you regained consciousness?'

He stared at her.

'Saying and doing what?'

She shrugged. 'Nothing terrible, I don't mean that. Just things like Dr Sanders dressing and bandaging your wound, helping you to the bathroom and into bed.'

'No, I don't remember that.'

'Well then isn't it possible... '

'You want to believe that's what my *father* did!'

'And *you* want to believe that he didn't!' She was becoming impatient with him.

'You'd like to think that he took care of me, but he didn't. I know he didn't! He can't even look after himself, for Christ's sake!'

She waited until his outburst was over.

'If I had a son like you, Tomas, and I discovered that he was gay...'

'*Queer* is the word,' he interrupted. 'Queer. I hate the word gay.'

'Queer, then.'

'Anyway, I didn't say that I was queer, did I?'

She was perplexed.

'No, but you said... '

'I asked you if the doctor said I was queer. And I told you what my father thinks about faggots. That's all.'

'Yes, that's what you said.'

He turned onto his side, scrutinising her, looking vulnerable.

'I don't know if I'm queer or not. Maybe that's worse.'

'Worse?'

'All I know is that I love Lorca.'

'Do you?'

'I do *know* what love is! What it feels like, what it does to you.'

'I believe you Tomas.'

'It's... it's all the rest of it I'm not so sure about.'

She nodded.

'We became friends when he was with Tamsyn, after Mother died. My father was unbearable most of the time, so she went and stayed with Lorca for the summer. He has his own flat in his parents' house. They're over twenty-one, so no one made a fuss about it. I was angry, but I couldn't blame her. She'd found someone and had somewhere to go. But I didn't, and I couldn't leave my father on his own.'

'No.'

'When Lorca went back to Exeter to start the autumn term she moved in with my grandparents.'

He sighed and shook his head. Jenna said nothing.

'I probably love him for the same reasons she does. At first it was his enthusiasm. He gets excited about just being alive in the world and wants to share it with everyone. But when you... when I got to know him, he's this quiet, gentle, loving man as well. He makes me believe in myself when we're together.'

'I'm glad for you, Tomas. I remember meeting you both at Exeter. He reminded me of my ministering angel.'

'Yes, he is! That night, after your reading, we went back to his digs, and I was so high on all the poetry. I read "Ministering Angel" to him. When I got to the lines about no one being able to hold him long, and never close enough, he knew what I meant – that I meant him. I don't know how he knew, how he knows most things, but he did. That was the first time we slept together. In his narrow little bed. Like... children.'

She waited a moment, but had to ask. 'What about Tamsyn?'

He looked at her. 'What about her? None of us has to choose between the other two, if that's what you mean.'

All at once an image blazed in Jenna's mind: Kitto on the terrace, at the pilchard palace, his back to her, smoking and silently brooding. It was their last long summer day together, with just one short night to come.

They both knew from the start that she would have to choose. Either it would be him – a new life for them both, which is what he said he wanted – or she would go back to Chyangwyns to begin a new chapter in her old life with Edward. When she started to tell him why she couldn't leave Edward he'd stormed outside.

She stood in the doorway, noticing the fine beads of perspiration that were forming on his tanned shoulders, his back, the cleavage of his paler buttocks.

He turned round, eyes glistening, his expression closed and detached – putting as much distance between them as he could until he was able to accept it and be with her again.

Tomas took another sip of water and lay back on the bed.

'When Lorca told me he was bisexual I didn't really know what it meant. I knew about it and had read about it, but I'd associated it with older men or married men, which was stupid. It starts when we're young. It has to, doesn't it? Everything does. The seeds of who we are don't suddenly burst into a different flower! A man or a woman doesn't turn into something else just because they get to a particular age or get married.'

'This is true.'

'I guess the word bisexual is okay, if it means some-where between two sexes. Like bimarian – your place between two seas.'

'I'm not so sure I like it. And I've gone off the word bimarian as well.'

'You have? Why?' He looked puzzled.

'I don't really know. It sounds too dry and clinical to me now. Like something you'd ask for at the chemist's. I should have just called the book *A Place Between Two Seas*, if that's what I meant.'

'But that wouldn't have been lipogramatic, would it?' There was a hint of mischief in his voice.

'No, it bloody well wouldn't!' She said this much louder than she'd intended, and saw the startled look on his face.

They continued staring at each other for a moment. Then they burst out laughing. They didn't stop until Jenna had a fit of coughing. He handed her the glass of water and she sipped from it until the coughing stopped.

'Why does everything have to be so complicated, Tomas?'

He shook his head.

'Love, friendship, language, learning – simply trying to live your own life and follow your own heart.'

'I know.'

'Even the word love – what we mean by it. Your love for Lorca and your sister and your mother. Your father. Each as different from the other as my love for Edward and Ester and Ebril. And Kitto.'

'Kitto?'

She nodded.

'In the midst of every battle in my life there's still my ministering angel.'

The flame in the lamp began to flutter. She leaned over and turned it down.

'I'm not good with ages, but is Kitto about thirty? With longish dark hair like me?'

She looked at him. 'Yes, and beautiful like you. Do you know him?'

'Not by name.'

'How, then?'

He smiled. 'We must like the same kind of weather. When a gale blows into the harbour I like to go sit on the quay. A couple of times he's been out there too. We've never spoken, but when you mentioned your ministering angel I suddenly got a picture of him.'

'How extraordinary.'

'He hasn't lived in Lamorna very long, has he?'

'No, and I haven't seen him for about... five months.'

'Didn't you see him today?'

'What?'

'That man going into The Wink. Wasn't that him?'

She opened her mouth, but couldn't think of anything to say. So she pressed her lips together and nodded.

They both fell silent.

'You know what I've been thinking, Tomas?'

She was looking wistfully at him.

'That loving can be the most difficult constraint of all, unless you accept the loneliness – the solitude, at least – that's always standing there in its shadow.'

Heavy drops of rain had begun splattering onto the skylight. After a moment's listening, Jenna realised that their conversation had come to an end.

'Have you thought about what you'd like to do tomorrow, Tomas?'

'No, but don't worry about me.'

He stretched his arms wide, yawning.

'You must have lots of things to catch up on. I can go for a walk in the morning. Maybe over to Carn Euny. And there's the fogou at Caer Brân. How far is Carn Euny from here? Ten minutes?'

'Maybe fifteen.'

'Lorca will be picking me up around three o'clock. He'll phone first.'

'Okay.'

She stood up.

'I'd better get off to bed. Digory will be up for his early morning run, whatever the weather.'

He tugged the duvet out from under him and pulled it up to his chin.

'Thank you,' he said, shyly.

'Thank *you*, Tomas.'

She felt an impulse to bend down and kiss him, on the cheek or forehead, but she didn't. Instead she turned off the lamp and left the room.

EIGHTEEN

The rain had blown over during the night, leaving a clean empty blue bowl of sky.

Jenna woke early and showered. She almost never wore make up, but studying her face in the misty mirror she decided that a little foundation and a touch of blusher would counter her paleness and the shadowy patches under her eyes. She decided to wear her green calf-length knitted dress with a chunky grey cardigan, because she had already made tentative plans for the day.

Digory followed her over to Chyangwyns to collect the post. Ester's car wasn't in the drive, so she'd already left for work.

Edward was in the kitchen, reading his newspaper over a cup of coffee.

'Morning, Jen. You're looking very smart.'

'Thanks.'

She picked up her post from the sideboard.

'I had a word with Postie this morning. He'll be delivering to The Fogou from tomorrow.'

'Thank you, Edward.'

He was still in his striped pyjamas and plaid robe. A dark blue and grey woollen scarf, which she recognised, was wrapped around his neck.

She had knitted that scarf for her father as a birthday present, three or four years ago. When they were sorting out his clothing, preparing for his move, she'd held it out for him to pack. He'd frowned and shaken his head, telling her he didn't need it. Ester immediately said she'd have it, and now Edward was wearing it. Had Ester given it to him? Or had theirs become the kind of relationship where he felt he could help himself to whatever she left lying about? But Ester wasn't someone who left anything lying about. Edward saw her gazing at it.

'I'm a bit chesty this morning.'

He put down the newspaper to tuck the scarf further under his pyjama collar. 'Might be coming down with a cold.'

'I hope not. Do you have any echinacea left?'

He looked bemused.

'I bought you some drops after Christmas, when you were feeling fluey, remember?'

'Oh, yes. They must be here somewhere.'

He glanced around the kitchen as though he might spot the bottle from where he sat.

She would leave it to him to look after himself – and of course Ester would be pleased to, if it did turn into a cold.

'How are you managing with the boy?'

'Fine. He'll be leaving this afternoon. I'll come over for supper tonight.'

'Good.'

'It's Tomas' birthday and I was thinking I'd take him to St Ives this morning. I could buy some sea bass and drop it by for Ester later this afternoon.'

'That would be lovely, Jen. Salt-baked sea bass.'

This didn't seem an appropriate moment to remind

him about collecting the eggs. She'd mention it this evening, or maybe it would be simpler if she just offered to take on the job herself.

'I'll bring over some rosemary and thyme as well.'

She turned to leave. Edward got up and followed her, as if he were seeing a visitor to the door, then gently kissed her goodbye. She could appreciate his kisses, dry and tender as they were these days. She preferred them to the rougher, gropey shows of affection he also had in his repertoire.

On her way back to The Fogou she wondered how many months or even years before Edward's illness her pleasure in their intimacy had begun to fade. Whenever it was, he'd already prematurely begun to show his age, his face becoming creased with wrinkles and losing the animated self-assurance it once wore. Perhaps she was partly to blame for that as well.

She took the several days' post to the sitting room table and looked through it all while the coffee brewed. In one envelope, pinned to a compliment slip from Moon Press, was her royalty cheque – much more than she'd expected. *Prismatic Vision* was still selling well since the Whitbread Prize, and so was *Bimarian Ground*, apparently.

Jenna decided that she would bake some muffins – a special birthday breakfast. She'd put on an apron and begun sifting the dry ingredients when Tomas appeared. Still wearing that nightshirt, and with his stubble of beard, she thought he looked like a young Jesus.

She smiled broadly. 'Happy Birthday, Tomas.'

He nodded, looking pleased and embarrassed.

'There's coffee in the pot.'

He poured himself a mug full, yawning. 'I had such amazing dreams.'

'So did I. Is it any wonder?'

The only residue she could recall from an early morning dream was a single image: Tomas asleep in a bed of straw in the guest room, with Ebril standing over him.

'In one of them I was flying or floating above The Fogou. I could see both coasts at once – Lamorna *and* Morvah. It was fantastic. Do you ever have flying dreams?'

'I used to.'

She remembered the dream diary she'd kept faithfully for a year, then abandoned when she realised how many of her dreams seemed to have something to do with motherhood.

He took his coffee into the conservatory. She caught up with him as he knelt to smell a newly opened gardenia blossom, holding the flower delicately between his fingers.

'They're so sweet-smelling.'

'Yes.'

'And such a soft whiteness.'

She watched him, enjoying his pleasure.

He stood and pointed to a row of tall plants at the back, with long spikes of drooping crimson flowers.

'What are those?'

She folded her arms. '*Amaranthus caudatus.*'

'What?'

'*Amaranthus* – from a Greek word that means unfading. The blossoms symbolise everlasting love and immortality.'

'Do they?'

'Love-lies-bleeding.'

He gave her a questioning look.

'Their common English name.'

'Much easier to remember.'

Tomas finished his coffee and she followed him back to the kitchen, a bit anxious.

'I hope I didn't sound like a botany teacher just then.'

He laughed, surprised. 'No! You sounded like a poet.'

'Good. I was thinking we could go to St Ives this morning.'

He looked curious. 'Okay. What did you want to do there?'

'Go to the Tate Gallery. Then have lunch somewhere? My treat.'

'All right.' He nodded. 'I'd like that.'

'Why don't you take a shower. I'll have breakfast ready in forty minutes.'

'Okay.'

'There's a fresh towel on the rail.'

'Thanks.'

'And, Tomas... '

He turned. 'Yes?'

'I think you can do without the bandage today.'

He smiled and nodded again.

When he came to the breakfast table Jenna was surprised at the difference a change of clothes could make to his appearance. In place of the faded flannel shirt and old corduroy trousers he'd been wearing for two days, he wore a green and mustard-coloured cross-striped cotton shirt and black jeans. It really suited him.

'Wow!'

'What?'

'You look terrific, Tomas.'

He flushed and pulled in his chair.

But it was more than the clothes. His long hair, still damp from the shower, seemed to be curling into ebony locks before her eyes, and the black stubble of beard gave him an almost rugged appearance. He was looking hungrily at the lemon and poppy seed muffins.

'And you look at least twenty years old.'

'Good. There's another revolting word gone.'

'What?'

She laughed at herself. 'Listen to me! You've got me saying it now – "*What!*" What word, Tomas?'

'Teen. Teenage.'

'Teenager. Teenaged,' she added.

'Teenybopper.'

They were enjoying themselves.

The muffins were warm enough for the butter to glisten as it melted into the cut halves.

'These are wonderful.' He ate half of one in two bites.

Jenna was pleased by his enthusiasm and their easy rapport this morning. She hadn't known what to expect when she woke up – anxious that this might turn into another day spent walking on eggshells. But watching him now, telling her about his extraordinary dream and illustrating it with animated gestures, there was a bright sparkle in his eyes, and she saw him in a completely fresh light.

It wasn't as if she'd forgotten last night and their arduous struggle – she never would. No, it was as though she was bearing witness to a transformation, from that confused, half-truculent, half-reticent boy into this more confident and mature young man sitting opposite her. Relaxed and unguarded, as he was now, he had a handsome face. She hadn't seen enough of it.

Tomas ate three muffins, and between them they finished off most of a second pot of coffee.

'God, I just remembered another dream.' He put his empty mug on his plate.

'Tell me.'

'I was... I'm not sure where. Sitting somewhere, naked, with my eyes closed.'

He looked uncertain for a moment, then continued.

'Anyway, I could feel this warm water washing over me. It went on and on, just a few pauses in between.'

'What do you… '

'I must have been dreaming about when I was little. While my mother bathed me and scrubbed me with a flannel she'd sing to me, or recite my favourite children's rhymes.'

He began to sound tentative. 'But all I could hear in my dream was… like breathing. It *was* breathing. So close, at first I thought it must be my own, but it wasn't. And… that's all I can remember.'

She began clearing the table. 'How strange.'

As they were about to leave, Edward dropped by to wish Tomas a happy birthday and he offered to have Digory while they were out.

'He never got his walk this morning,' she told him. 'Would you have time to take him for a run?'

He tugged at his scarf. 'I'm sure we can manage a mile or two. Fresh air will do me good.'

She went to the kitchen, ostensibly to collect Digory's collar and lead, although he wouldn't actually need it. She was curious to know what Tomas and Edward would make of each other today, and took her time. When she eventually rejoined them, Tomas was telling Edward about her *Selected Verses* being in the A-level English syllabus.

'We studied them all last term. Everyone got really into them,' he was saying, 'and not just because she's a local celebrity. Anyone in my class would have jumped at the chance to meet your wife and do the interview. Unfortunately, she got lumbered with me!'

Edward chuckled, clearly impressed.

NINETEEN

They set off for St Ives at ten-thirty. There were few direct roads through West Penwith, but hundreds of miles of narrow winding lanes and unmade tracks that only seemed to exist in order to connect one small isolated settlement to the next. Artery roads like this one skirting Zennor were barely wide enough or straight enough to contain the flow of traffic, except sometimes in winter. It was all too easy to pass through this extraordinary land with eyes narrowly focussed on the road or the vehicle in front, without even noticing the strange beauty of these places.

Jenna was taking in everything, and Tomas, silently watchful, was equally absorbed in where they were. 'Glorious!' she exclaimed, shaking her head as they rounded yet another sharp bend and began descending between tidy fields and sweeping moorland. He felt no need to add an *amen* to this particular moment in their lives.

They parked at the harbour quay, walked through the Warren and out onto Porthmeor Beach.

Tomas strolled ahead, pausing now and then to look out across the bay towards Godrevy Lighthouse. He'd left his cap and gloves in the car, and his unbuttoned coat was blowing open.

When Jenna stopped to tuck her hair under her beret she watched him, admiring his solidity, the self-assurance in his gait, compared to yesterday and the day before. Again she marvelled at how he had physically and emotionally matured over their brief time together, and could now rightfully claim his twenty years.

The Tate was relatively uncrowded. They spent nearly half the morning meandering through its galleries together. At one point, Jenna stood for many minutes contemplating a vibrant still life by Winifred Nicholson. Tomas found himself virtually drawn into Christopher Wood's lyrical little harbour scene, and before they left he had to return to it for one last look.

Outside, the bright piercing light made them blink as they stood on the top step, looking out over the strand. Jenna stole a sideways glance at Tomas and could guess from his expression that being here on a brilliant winter day was something he hadn't experienced before.

'Come on.' She grabbed his arm.

They crossed the road to the seafront and walked side by side along the tide line. After ambling down Bunkers Hill to Wharf Road, she steered them up a couple of steps onto a café veranda and chose a harbour-side table for them.

'Cappuccino, *monsieur*?' she asked.

'*Oui, madame.*'

She told the waitress, '*Deux cappuccino, s'il vous plâit.*'

Tomas grinned, looking at all the empty tables. 'Café society! Probably as close as I'll ever get to Paris.'

'We Aquarians don't need to travel much,' she replied sedately. 'This is far enough for today. *Tu es d'accord?*'

'*D'accord.*'

'You learnt French at school?'

'Studied French. Didn't learn a lot.'

They looked out at the harbour, where most of the boats were tilting against the ebbing tide.

'I'd like to get to the second-hand bookshop,' he told her. 'Lorca says it's a good one. Do we have time?'

'Plenty of time. I need to go to the fishmongers and do one or two other errands. We can go our separate ways for an hour and... '

Their coffees arrived.

'*Merci*... we can meet up at the bookshop in an hour.'

'Okay.'

'I've been meaning to ask you what Lorca's studying at Exeter.'

'It's a combined BA degree in English and Film Studies.'

'I'm impressed. And what will you do?'

'If I get in, you mean? I want to do the BA in English, with study in North America. I'd spend my second year at a university there – hopefully, the College of William and Mary in Virginia.'

'That would be wonderful!'

'Yes. If it happens.'

'I'm sure it will.'

'My grandmother's brother-in-law's an American. He says he'd help financially. And some of his family in the States would sponsor me.'

'Then it's meant to be, isn't it? We Aquarians can travel far when we're determined.'

After paying the bill, Jenna told Tomas the way to the bookshop and they went off in opposite directions.

But going from place to place, completing her shopping quickly and then hurrying along the narrow streets that wind through Upalong, Jenna felt increasingly uneasy. When she finally realised the source of her anxiety she stopped in her tracks. She had left Tomas on his own, out of doors, for the first time in three days. What if he became confused again? Disorientated? Got himself lost or just disappeared?

She looked out at the boats in the harbour, now abandoned by the tide, trying to reassure herself that – for heaven's sake – this was the same solid, clear-headed young man she'd been admiring all morning. He wasn't going to suddenly vanish from her life. Not yet, anyway.

When she arrived at the bookshop Tomas wasn't there. She couldn't possibly go browsing through the shelves, not knowing where he was. She felt too flustered to simply ask the salesperson if he'd been there, so she stood frozen near the door and waited for five long minutes before hurrying back outside.

She retraced her steps down the granite stairway, through the little alleyway and out onto the pavement. Where should she go? Or should she just wait here and hope? She looked up the road, then down the road, one way, then the other, until she worried that her behaviour might be attracting attention. So she sat on the bench in front of the bookshop, watching without seeing anyone in the stream of people passing by. She nervously adjusted her parcels, trying to catch her breath, and eventually she just stared, motionless, across the road. Tears were beginning to accumulate in the corners of her eyes.

She didn't notice Tomas approaching. When he slumped down close beside her on the bench, smiling, she let out a cry.

He saw the anguish in her face.

'What? What is it?'

She bowed her head.

'Jenna?'

She looked up at him in astonishment.

'Do you know, that's the first time you've actually spoken my name in three days, Tomas.'

'Is it?'

'I think it is.'

'And that's what's upsetting you? That I haven't been calling you Jenna?'

They both laughed.

She had to confess, tell him every detail – all the irrational thoughts that had plagued her over the past hour.

'When I got to the bookshop I couldn't believe you weren't there, and I panicked again. So stupid!'

'I was there for forty-five minutes, then went back to a shop up the road that sells... '

'It's all right, Tomas, you don't have to explain. This was all my own... craziness.' She shook her head.

They continued to sit, silent now, for another minute.

'You must be as hungry as I am.'

He nodded.

'Where shall we go then?'

He looked uncertain. 'You decide.'

'I will not. It's your birthday!'

'Okay. What about a pizza, back at the café?'

'An excellent choice.'

This last meal together was just as Jenna had hoped. They sat indoors, at a bright sun-lit table right at the front, taking their time exploring the menu. By the time their pizzas came out of the wood-fired oven and were brought to the table to join the salads and drinks, it had turned into an outstanding occasion for them both, finishing in servings of chocolate and orange torte.

'How will you be presenting our interview to your class, Tomas?'

'Good question... Jenna.'

She smiled, telling him that he'd made a very good second go at using her name.

'I'll write up what I can remember about Sunday. I should have taken notes.'

'You weren't well.'

'Some of what you said's been coming back to me, though. And yesterday... well I remember all of yesterday. Anyway, it'll have to be as good as I can make it, because it becomes part of my overall English grade. I'll hand it in to the teacher, then she'll copy and distribute it for class discussion and comments.'

'But we didn't really discuss my *Selected Verses*, Tomas.'

'No, not directly... '

'Look, we'll have some time when we get back. Why don't we sit down with the book and you can ask me questions about any of the poems and take some notes?'

He shook his head. 'I couldn't ask you to do that.'

'You're not asking, I'm offering.'

'If you're sure. That would be great.'

Over coffee she asked him what he'd bought at the bookshop. Sheepishly, he slid a paperback out of the bag. It was a well-worn anthology, published by Moon Press, entitled *New Cornish Poets*. It included a dozen of Jenna's earliest verses.

'I've never seen it before. It has some of your poems I haven't read.'

She took it from him and self-consciously leafed through its pages.

'Dear God! I haven't seen this in years. It makes me feel old, knowing I can be found on second-hand bookshelves.'

As he was putting it back into the bag she held out her hand.

'Let me have it again.' She took a pen from her handbag, opened the book to the first blank page and wrote something onto it before handing it back to him.

He read:

> *Dear Tomas,*
> *Never forget the day when two travelling*
> *companions journeyed through St Ives,*
> *together on their separate ways:*
> *The Sixteenth of February.*
> *Remember me. I will always remember you.*
> *Love,*
> *Jenna.*

Looking up, his eyes brimmed with tears. She reached for his hand, but he was rummaging though his bag and brought out something else.

'This is for you.'

He handed her a diary. Its cover design, front and back, was row upon row of alternating blood red and grass green hearts.

'It's a bit garish, but you won't easily lose it.'

'How did you know?'

'You told me yesterday. During one of our shouting matches.'

'Did I?'

'One of *my* shouting matches.'

She flipped through the pages. 'No, I won't lose this one. Thank you, Tomas.'

He gave her his hand.

TWENTY

When they arrived back at The Fogou, Tomas offered to wash up the breakfast things. Jenna was putting a pad of lined paper, some pens and her *Selected Verses* on the sitting room table when her phone rang.

She recognised the voice, which was warm and cheerful.

'Good afternoon, Ms Mundey, this is Lorcan McCall speaking.'

'Yes, hello, Lorcan.'

'I'll be collecting Tomas around three o'clock, if that's all right with you.'

She glanced at her watch. 'I wonder, would three-thirty be possible instead?'

'Yes, that would be fine.'

'Should I give you directions here?'

'Tomas has told me where you are. I'm sure I'll find you, but thanks.'

'We'll see you soon, then.'

'Would you give him a short message from me, please?'

'You can speak to him yourself if you like. He's just in the kitchen.'

'Doing the washing up, is he?'

'As a matter of fact he is!'

They both laughed.

'Hold on, Lorcan.'

She took the phone to Tomas. He dried his hands and took it.

She went out of the kitchen door, lifted one of the two tin ash boxes by its handle and carried it around to the sitting room. She emptied the ashes from the stove into it, put kindling into the firebox and positioned two fat logs on top before lighting it. As she was heading towards the door, Tomas came through.

'Let me take that.'

He took the box from her. 'Back outside the kitchen door?'

'No, let's take it round to the garden.'

She held the door for him, opened and closed the back gate after them and followed him along the cinder path.

'Here by the tap is fine.'

He set it down.

She had her arms crossed, inspecting the garden with a critical eye.

'Did you make all this yourself?' he asked.

'Yes I did. Creating a garden from scratch is a huge responsibility. Very different from filling a conservatory with exotic ready-mades.'

He looked around, noticing that the low box hedges enclosed not only herb beds, but young perennial plants, bulbs, rhizomes and corms, some of them already in flower.

'It all looks so new and tentative,' she told him.

'Well, it *is* new!'

'I was tempted to plant everything closer together – to give the garden a fuller feeling right at the start.' She leant over a hedge and picked several sprigs of rosemary. A bit further on she pinched off a few top stems of lemon thyme. 'But if I had done I would have denied these young ones the space and light they'll need if they're going to flourish.'

'Fulfil their potential,' he added.

She turned to him and threaded a stem of rosemary through the top buttonhole of his coat. Patting it down, she grinned at him. 'Exactly.'

He tapped the ash box with his foot. 'What are you going to do with this?'

'I'll put the wood ash around the perennials, to keep the slugs at bay.'

'Would you like me to...?'

'No, I'll do it later, thanks. We don't have that much time. Let's go and get Digory.'

They walked around the back of the barn and onto the farm track.

'I've got some good news,' he said.

'Tell me.'

'Lorca's going to be at Longrock for five days and he's invited me to stay there.'

'Oh, what a relief for you!'

'Not just until he goes back to Exeter. His parents say they're happy for me to stay in his flat for as long as I need it. Until summer, at least.'

'Tomas, that's incredible news!'

'It is, isn't it?'

'I'm so happy for you!'

They'd stopped walking. She resisted the impulse for as long as she could, and then hugged him. It was a short, self-conscious embrace, but it was enough.

'I told Lorca I'd give his parents rent money, but he said as long as the utilities are paid for they won't want anything else.'

'You'll be able to manage that?'

'Yeah, look.'

He reached into his back pocket and took out the bundle of twenty pound notes. 'Most of last summer's wages.'

Ester and Edward were in the study, hunched over the computer screen, scrutinising a spreadsheet. They stopped their bickering immediately.

Ester switched off the screen and stood smiling at Tomas. 'Happy Birthday to You,' she crooned, which made Digory bark. 'How's your day been so far?'

'Glorious!'

There was the same enthusiasm in his voice as there had been in Jenna's benediction when they were on their way to St Ives.

'Herbs.' Jenna presented her sister with the green bouquet. 'I'll bring the bass over in a bit.'

'No hurry.'

Much to everyone's surprise, as they were saying their goodbyes, Tomas shook their hands – first Ester's, then Edward's – and warmly thanked them.

As soon as they were through the gate in the yew hedge, Tomas took from his coat pocket a heart-shaped dog biscuit as large as his hand. Digory saw it, too.

'Wherever did you get that?' Jenna asked in amazement.

'A shop in St Ives. It's got no sugar in it – I asked. Can he have it?'

'Yes, he'll love it.'

Digory stood on his hind legs, delicately took the biscuit from him, then turned and trotted off.

'Whenever I went to visit my grandparents I'd bring their Jack Russell one of those. She'd bury it in the garden somewhere, and when she dug it up later she'd pretend she'd found it, all by herself.'

They watched Digory disappearing behind the barn.

'I'd better go and pack. I'll just be a minute.' He walked on ahead.

'Your Levertov book's still on the table in the library,' she shouted after him.

Watching him open the kitchen door and then slam it behind him, she thought, *As though he's at home.*

Sitting at the bay window, both of them concentrating on the task and aware of the limited time they had, the interview was focussed, had enough depth to it, and was surprisingly successful.

'I've got more than enough here,' he told her, looking through his notes.

She was about to offer to read a draft of his essay and give him feedback before he handed it in, but she stopped herself.

'Good luck with it, Tomas.'

'Thanks. I'll send you a copy if you'd like to have it.'

'Yes, of course I would! And... '

'What?'

'When you've finished your sonnet, if that's what it becomes, would you send me a copy of that as well?'

He considered for a few seconds. 'Only if it's good enough. Is that okay?'

'Yes, that's fair enough.'

'If it's not, I'll send you one or two that might be.'

Jenna decided that when Lorca arrived she wouldn't invite him in for a cup of tea. It wasn't that she felt in any way unfriendly toward him or wouldn't welcome the opportunity to meet him again. She'd made this decision out of consideration for Tomas. She suspected, although she might be wrong, that when the moment came Tomas would want to leave her and Digory and The Fogou on his own. The word she was searching for and eventually found was 'closure'.

She had made a pot of tea and they were standing at the kitchen counter drinking it. She picked up a large envelope from her pile of mail and took out sheets of green printed paper – fliers advertising her poetry reading in Cardiff.

'These came this morning. What do you think?'

Tomas took one, read it, folded it into quarters and slipped it into his back pocket.

'I'll see you there.'

'It's a long way to go for just an evening, Tomas. I'd offer you a lift, but I'm not... '

'It's okay,' he assured her. 'I'll break the journey at Exeter. Coming and going.'

Digory scratched at the door and she let him in. His nose and front paws were smudged with soil.

They sat in the sitting room for a quarter of an hour, hardly making conversation, before they heard the rumble of a motorcycle pulling into the yard.

They got up. Tomas pulled his rucksack over his shoulder while Jenna stood in the open doorway.

He embraced her, holding her tightly against his chest. 'Jenna... '

She kissed him hard on the cheek, hesitated, then kissed him on the other cheek before pushing him away.

She closed the door and went to the window to watch him greeting Lorca. He said something she couldn't hear, but Lorca laughed and reached out to tousle his hair. Tomas grabbed the hand and held onto it, gesturing toward the wound at the back of his head.

Lorca handed him a crash helmet, which he carefully eased over his head.

They both mounted the motorcycle. As Lorca looked behind them, revving the engine and turning the bike around, Jenna watched Tomas' arms slide further around his friend's leather-jacketed waist. In a moment they were gone.

Digory was still sniffing and whining at the door. She called him to her and tenderly stroked his head.

'Yes, he's gone, Digory. Whatever shall we do now?'

ENVOI

It was nearly dark by the time they arrived at the well. Jenna sat on the bottom step, gazing into the shallow pool of water, struggling to clear her mind of every irrelevant thought.

After a few minutes she felt she had absorbed something of the stillness, the sweet silence of the place, and was grateful.

As always, she wanted to offer something back. It would never be one of her own verses – she felt that would be egotistical. But choosing something appropriate for the specific occasion of each visit wasn't easy. She would never try to force it, or become impatient when it wouldn't emerge out of the hundreds of verses she knew by heart. Now it did come: lines from Levertov's 'A Dream of Cornwall'.

She whispered:

> 'O fear dissolves here and now I cease
> to hear the hammer the axe the bone the bell,
> shade of a shade grown still, grief of a grief
> lulled in green hollows of a well of peace.'

She rejoined Digory, who had been standing on the top step, watching and listening.

Her purple cloutie still hung on the thorn tree, with Tomas' daffodil tied to it. The flower was wilted and turning brown now.

She took the paisley handkerchief from her pocket. She'd found it under Tomas' pillow when she was stripping the bedding from the futon in the guest room an hour ago. She held it either side of a torn corner, intending to tear off a strip and tie it next to their last offerings. She could make another half dozen clouties from his handkerchief – enough to last until Easter if she visited the well every week.

But now she changed her mind and tucked it back into her pocket.

Jenna put Digory's bowl onto his mat, opened the kitchen door and loudly called, 'Digory! Supper!'

He came in carrying the biscuit Tomas had given him, set it on the mat next to his water bowl and ate his supper while she watched him.

'My goodness, Digs – buried treasure for afters! Aren't you lucky?'

It was then that she decided what to do with the handkerchief.

Today's visit to the well was enough to remember their friendship over the past three days. In future she would only go there for herself and her own needs, as she had always done. Tomas could do the same, if he still lived close enough. If not, no doubt he would find other sources to inspire him, as young poets have always done.

She took the handkerchief from her pocket, spread it out on the counter and folded it neatly into a square.

Digory followed her into the sitting room and lay on the braided rug in front of the stove to eat his biscuit.

She lifted the empty heart-shaped wooden box from its shelf and placed Tomas' handkerchief inside. There it would stay, unless he realised he had lost it and came back to claim it. But she felt quite certain that he wouldn't.

ABOUT THE AUTHOR

R D Cook was a founding member of staff at Brockwood Park School in Hampshire. He then trained as a therapist and developed and managed a range of intensive programmes for serious offenders with the Probation Service. He also worked as supervisor of counselling and trainer with several Westminster Pastoral Foundation affiliated services, and was a freelance groupwork trainer and part-time university lecturer. He and his wife, a painter and gardener, live on a smallholding in North Pembrokeshire. They have one daughter.

ACKNOWLEDGEMENTS

William Carlos Williams

Asphodel, That Greeny Flower
First published in *Journey to Love* (1955)
Copyright © 1962 William Carlos Williams/New Directions
Publishing Corporation, New York

Denise Levertov

Relearning the Alphabet
Published in *New Selected Poems* by Bloodaxe Books Ltd,
2003. First published in the USA in 2002 in *Selected Poems*
by New Directions Publishing Corporation, New York

The Wedding Ring
Published in *New Selected Poems* by Bloodaxe Books Ltd
2003. First published in the USA in 2002 in *Selected Poems*
by New Directions Publishing Corporation, New York

The Dreamers
From *Collected Earlier Poems 1940-1960*, published by
New Directions Publishing Corporation, New York, 1979

A Gift
First published in *Sands of the Well* by New Directions
Publishing Corporation, New York, 1998

The Métier of Blossoming
Published in *New Selected Poems* by Bloodaxe Books Ltd
2003. First published in the USA in 2002 in *Selected Poems*
by New Directions Publishing Corporation, New York

The Disclosure
Published in *New Selected Poems* by Bloodaxe Books Ltd
2003. First published in the USA in 2002 in *Selected Poems*
by New Directions Publishing Corporation, New York

A Dream of Cornwall
From *Collected Earlier Poems, 1940-1960*, published by
New Directions Publishing Corporation, New York, 1979

Emily Dickinson

The Complete Poems, Faber and Faber, 1976